LUMBERJACK

DAN GARLAND

LUMBERJACK

BY STEPHEN W. MEADER

ILLUSTRATED BY HENRY C. PITZ

ISBN 978-1-931177-20-7 cloth
ISBN 978-1-931177-21-4 paperback

SOUTHERN SKIES

LITTLE ROCK, ARKANSAS
www.southernskies.com

Dedication

The republication of this book is dedicated with love to William Lane Chandler Kidd by his "Papa Jerry," Jerry Atchley.

FOREWORD

TWENTY-FIVE years ago, when I was growing up in New Hampshire, my father owned a portable sawmill, operating in near-by counties and across the line in Maine. Among my most enjoyable memories are those of weeks I spent with him in camp—driving up behind a fast trotter—sleeping in a shanty on wheels—eating with the lumberjacks—helping the teamsters with their sure-footed woods-horses.

Father's business was cutting timber. But I think he never laid the ax to a fine stand of pine without a feeling of regret. And certainly no one ever appreciated the beauty of a living forest more than he. Today his greatest pride is the 300-acre lot where his own white pines grow taller and sturdier every year.

To him and his vivid recollection of sawmill days I owe much of the detail in this book. Lumbering, in southern Maine and New Hampshire, has changed very little in the last generation. The pines still flourish, in spite of neglect and forest fires and the more recent attacks of white pine blister—the enemy that lurks in wild-gooseberry bushes. In many parts of

New England, reforestation projects are bringing back the glory of standing timber and restoring the value of waste-lands.

But the fast-stepping horses of my boyhood are gone from the roads. Today, if you want to see beauty of motion that no machine can ever match, you must go to a County Fair track and watch the harness races.

Most of the stories told by Judge Garland in these pages are actual legends of the countryside. Some of them are taken from *New Hampshire Folk Tales,* a delightful book published by the New Hampshire Federation of Women's Clubs. Others, like the one about Uncle Lemmie and the bear, are stories that have been told for generations in my own family. The "starving year" is authentic history, and people around the neighborhood still tell of a buried hoard of silver dollars, never discovered to this day.

Stephen W. Meader

March 7, 1934

ILLUSTRATIONS

LUMBERJACK

I

A CHEERFUL radiance seeped through the closed lids of Dan Garland's eyes and warned him that it was time to get up. He stretched luxuriously and rose on one elbow. Every corner of his little room under the eaves was flooded with golden light. It was a pleasant room to wake up in, at any time of year. All summer three big sugar maples beside the house screened the east window with deep, cool green. Now, in October, their yellow and scarlet foliage gave a ruddy glow to the morning sun.

That warm color was deceptive, as Dan found when he threw back the bedclothes. There was a nip in the air. Football weather, he thought, with a twinge of

3

longing. No gridiron thrills for him this fall. He was a working man.

Swiftly he got into his clothes, pulled on his overalls and stable-boots and hustled down the stairs. A wave of warm enticing smells flowed from the big kitchen but he resisted its lure. Out in the yard the frosty grass was crisp under his feet. What little air was stirring came out of the northwest, where the mountains rose in bold, blue outline.

It was comfortable in the barn. Babe, the little black mare, neighed softly from her box-stall. Judy, the venerable Jersey, rattled the stanchion with her horns, and blew out her breath in a long, sweet-scented sigh. Climbing to the loft, Dan threw down forkfuls of hay and fed them both. Then from a dusty corner he brought the old three-legged stool, home-made of solid hickory and worn smooth by three generations of Garland milkers. Settling the brightly scoured pail between his knees, he thrust his forehead into the hollow of Judy's flank and went to work. It wasn't a long job. Four or five quarts of yellow milk was all the old cow gave, morning and night. But it sufficed for their small household, and produced enough cream for butter, besides.

At seven o'clock Dan had stripped the last drops

into the pail. He left Judy browsing on corn-fodder in the barnyard and went in to breakfast.

"F'heaven's sakes set yer milk right there, 'n' git off them overhauls," a high, rapid voice greeted him. "Yer grandpa's already at table, an' there's popovers fer breakfast."

"Okay, Debbie," Dan grinned. "I'll be there while they're hot."

Swiftly the little old woman pumped a basin of water for him, and he scrubbed his forearms and soused his face. He didn't mind Debbie Hicks' sharp ways. She had been keeping house for Judge Garland for thirty years, and managed things with a high hand. But she knew what boys liked to eat.

He went into the dining-room and greeted his grandfather. The Judge sat in his big chair at the head of the table, a napkin tied around his neck.

"Well, Danny," he chuckled, "found it jest a mite brisk outside, this mornin', didn't you?"

"There was frost all right," the boy replied. "Debbie's flowers are done for, this year."

The old man chuckled again. He was feeling good this morning. Eager and intent on something. Dan looked at him appreciatively. No one would have guessed his grandfather was eighty years old. He was a round little man of sturdy build, his rosy countenance framed by silver hair and a short, white, pointed beard. From the corners of his twinkling blue eyes, a network of fine lines radiated. His face made Dan think of a wrinkled winter apple, sound and sweet, and rimed with frost.

Judge Garland had never really occupied the Bench. But for many years he had been a local Justice of the Peace, and the townspeople of Green Hill and Riverdale spoke of him always as "the Judge."

The silence that prevailed while they ate their bacon and eggs and balloon-like, golden-brown popovers, was broken suddenly by Dan's grandfather.

"Ben Buckalew's comin' today," he announced briskly.

"Ben Buckalew?" asked Dan. "Oh—the sawmill man? Gee, Grandpa, you're not serious about cutting that timber, are you?"

"Jest as plumb serious as I ever was in my life," twinkled the old man. "In fact, it's all settled. Them pines have stood there long enough. Most of 'em are mighty near as old as I am, an' they've never done a hand's turn o' work fer me all these years I've supported 'em. Now it's time for 'em to show their gratitude."

"I know," said Dan soberly. "But there isn't a stand of pine like it in the state. When you walk through and see 'em standing up so tall and straight —why, it's like a church. Seems as if it would be a sin to cut down all that beauty—"

"Nonsense," his grandfather laughed. "Nobody's any fonder o' that timber-lot than I am. But pshaw! It'll come back. A couple o' generations an' the Garland pines'll be jest as famous as ever. Besides— what's the good o' havin' 'em if we don't use 'em. You're goin' to college, boy, an' they're goin' to send you there!"

Thoughtfully, Dan buttered another popover. "I wish there was some other way," he said, and meant it. "Soon as I get a job I ought to save three or four hundred dollars this winter. With that for a back-log I could work my way through. I know a chap that's doing it at Dartmouth right now."

"Thunderation!" rumbled the Judge. "Can't I have my own way once in a while? I've been lookin' forward to the fun of cuttin' them pines a long time. Turn 'em into lumber an' they're money in the bank. Leave 'em there an' maybe a forest fire comes along. Then what have you got? Why, Danny, for forty years I've been as nervous as a cow with her first calf, every time I smelt smoke!"

There was no answering the common sense of this argument. Dan folded his napkin and went back to the barn, his heart still heavy. It would be grand to go to college—to give his attention to books and football without worrying about money. But he still felt like a murderer every time he thought of laying the ax to those strong, tall, graceful trees.

Morning chores at the Garland place didn't take long. Dan could have finished in half an hour if he had been in a hurry, but on this day he preferred to do his work slowly and thoroughly. Warm sun came flooding through the open south door, and hens clucked contentedly in the barnyard. Dan cleaned out the stalls with care, and brought armfuls of fresh straw from the mow. Then he moved in beside the little black trotter.

Playfully she nuzzled at his hand with her mouse-gray nose, turning her shapely head to the limit of the halter. He patted her flank.

"Move over there, you black honey, and stop your flirting," he laughed. "Don't you know I'm just your lady's maid?" He took curry-comb and brush from the rack and went to work on her slim, round barrel. The mare loved it. She arched her neck and pawed lightly with one dainty forefoot as the boy's hands alternately rasped and sleeked her coat. When every shining hair lay smoothly in place he rubbed down the slender legs, polishing each hoof with a touch of axle-grease. Then he brushed out her tail into a billowy black cloud. And last of all he groomed her head and neck, working over the flowing mane and the clipped forelock.

Dan finished and stepped back to admire his handiwork. The sun came in a south window to gleam on Babe's shimmering black flank. The mare, he thought with a smile, was as beautiful and almost as youthfully slender as she looked in that photograph over the desk in the Judge's office. She had been a filly then, in her first year of racing. "Jerusha Dillon—2:08¼" was the lettering engraved on a brass plate beneath the picture. Dan remembered the day she came to Green Hill—a gaunt, dust-coated scarecrow of a horse, limping slowly behind the veterinary's buggy.

It was when she was a four-year-old—in her second year on the County Fair tracks—that the accident had happened. Judge Garland, always an inveterate harness-racing fan, had seen it. He was leaning on the rail at the last turn—the spot from which he always watched a trotting-match. It was the third heat. The little black mare had been boxed in the first, but had come through to win the second handily. Her owner and driver, old Ray Newton, had kept her wide on the back-stretch and around the upper curve. Then, seeing his chance, he cut for the pole and let the mare out. A hard-faced 'York State driver, whose big bay horse had won the first heat, was still ahead when they came into the straightaway. But he was well out from the rail, and old Ray headed the mare for the opening, going like the wind. As her reaching nose crept abreast of the sulky the other driver sawed on his reins and the bay broke, swinging disconcertingly to the left. There was a crash and a cloud of dust. The little mare's foreleg had struck the swerving sulky wheel and she was thrown heavily against the fence. Somehow Ray Newton climbed out of the wreckage with only a few scratches. The 'York State driver was barred from the track, and that ended the incident as far as the newspapers were concerned.

But for Judge Garland and his grandson it was only the beginning of the story. When the little black trotter had been untangled from the broken shafts and pulled to her feet it was obvious that she was through with racing. One foreleg was wrenched at the shoulder and bleeding from a deep cut below the knee. She was barely able to hobble off the track. Newton, looking at her disgustedly in the paddock, jumped at the old Judge's offer of a hundred dollars.

Grandfather Garland often told about it with a

chuckle. "Looked at me like he thought I was plumb crazy. Wouldn't believe it till I put the bills in his hand. Then he begun to be sorry for me! 'Judge,' he said, 'I ain't one to take advantage of an old friend. I hate to see ye stuck like this. I was aimin' to destroy her, an' that's a fact!' But, Danny, I wasn't the dotin' old fool he must ha' figgered me. For a fifth o' what she was worth I got a four-year-old trotter that turned out to be the best road-hoss in the county, an' has been, fer goin' on ten years."

Only Dan—a little boy when the mare had been brought home—knew the weeks of patient nursing that Judge Garland and the vet from Riverdale gave that injured leg. By the time snow flew, Jerusha Dillon was her easy-gaited self again. But the Judge had never liked her first name. From that day on she was known to the countryside as "Babe." And though she was in her fourteenth year now, there were few horses that could keep her dust in sight on the highroad.

Dan went out to the chicken-house on the far side of the barnyard and fed the Rhode Island Reds. Then, his chores over, he walked slowly back to the house. The white frame structure under the maples had been his home ever since he was five. He was the last of the Garland line. Orphaned by an epidemic that swept the New York suburb where he lived, he was brought back to Green Hill by his grandfather and turned over to Debbie's brisk but kindly ministrations.

Together they had raised him, put him through High School in Riverdale, and now they were planning to send him to college. There wasn't a very big income from the Judge's savings. Dan had realized that for years. He had worked hard, summers, to earn enough for clothes, and he did everything he could around the place to pay for his keep. Now his grandfather was going to cut the Garland pines, and the boy knew he was doing it for him.

As he reached the kitchen porch, he heard a quick clop-clop of hoofs coming up the road. Singing wheels turned in at the gate and crunched on the gravel beside the house.

"Who-o-oah, boy!" murmured a low-pitched voice.

Dan stepped around the corner and saw a big roan horse and a yellow-wheeled buggy standing in the driveway. The horse's strawberry hide was darkened with wet patches and when he tossed his head, flecks of yellow foam flew from the bit.

The single occupant of the buggy jumped nimbly out, over the wheel, and came forward with a hitching-rope in his hand. He was a broad-shouldered man with a weathered, square face and hair that was grizzled at the temples. A pair of steely gray eyes looked out at Dan from under jutting brows.

"Morning," said the stranger briefly. "My name's Buckalew. Where'll I find the Judge?"

II

JUDGE GARLAND had come bustling to the door in his carpet-slippers even before Dan could show Buckalew the hitching-post.

"Come in, Ben—come in!" he called heartily. "Been expectin' you this half hour. What kept you? Old roan slowin' up a mite?"

Buckalew's eyes crinkled at the corners.

"Same old joker, ain't ye?" he snorted in mock anger. "No, I can't say I've noticed any fallin' off in his speed. Matter o' fact I was gittin' ready to brag a little about the time we made this mornin'."

He pulled out a massive silver watch. "Only a couple o' minutes over two hours fer the trip," he announced. "Twenty-two mile, ain't it—from the Maine state line? An' I live two mile further. Call it twelve mile an hour, which you'll admit is pretty fair fer these miserable New Hampshire roads."

It was the Judge's turn to show his ire.

"Best roads north o' Boston!" he declared hotly. "But come on inside, while I put on some shoes. We'll start pretty soon—though I expect that hoss o' yours really needs a rest. Two hours *is* good time, I'll grant. Did you hear 'bout the city feller that made it from the state line in an hour 'n' a quarter with one of them new-fangled gasoline kerridges? Fact! I heard it down to the store last week."

"Them contraptions is fast," Buckalew allowed grudgingly, as he was shown into the little office back of the parlor. "They'll never take the place o' hosses, though. Too durn dangerous an' undependable!"

"Right now they are," the older man agreed. "Lucky to run a mile without breakin' down. Smell terrible, too. Worse'n a skunk. But don't you be too surprised if they really turn out to be somethin' in a few years."

The Judge pushed forward a chair. "Ben," he said,

"I don't b'lieve you've met my grandson. Danny, shake hands with the best mill-man in the country."

Buckalew thrust out a calloused palm and Dan gripped it with a grin. The steel-gray eyes appraised him keenly.

"Big, fer a Garland, ain't he?" asked the lumber-man.

"His mother's folks was tall men," beamed the Judge. "Guess he's close to five-foot-eleven, an' still a couple o' years to grow."

For a few moments the two men discussed the weather, politics, and the price of lumber, sawed and on the stump. Then Judge Garland pulled on his boots and donned hat and overcoat.

"Hitch up, Danny," he said. "We'll be gittin' over to the lot."

Harnessing Babe was a pleasure. She was always eager to get out on the road and never offered objections to taking the bit or having the girth buckled. In two or three minutes Dan had her between the shafts of the light road-wagon and led her around to the house. The tall roan whinnied as she approached and pawed nervously at the gravel.

Grandpa took the driver's seat, with Dan beside him. "I'd better go first, an' show you the way," he told Buckalew. In a moment both rigs had swung out of the yard and were spinning up the road to the north.

It was only two miles and a half to the upper farm. The narrow track wound up through a fold in the hills and over the crest of a rise. There a white gate opened to the left. They bowled between the gate-posts and into the yard of a rambling gray farmhouse.

"Hello there! Jotham Grant!" called the Judge. The tenant farmer answered from the barn and came out to greet them. He was a big, slow-moving, stoop-shouldered man with a kindly smile behind his brown beard. Dan got out and hitched the horses while the men talked.

A tousle-headed boy of eleven emerged from the wood-shed that connected house and barn. He wore a rugged home-knit sweater and overalls, tucked into cowhide boots. A big buff and white collie moved quietly beside him.

"Hi, Dan," the boy grinned shyly.

"Hi, 'Lysses," said Dan. "How's the woodchuck crop?"

"Got four more, since you was here," Ulysses replied. "Look. There's the skins!"

On the open shed door, sure enough, four gray hides were stretched.

"The big one, I shot," the boy explained with pride. "Jack killed the rest."

"He's some dog!" said Dan approvingly. "What are you going to do with the hides?"

"Dunno," Ulysses frowned. "They ain't worth nothin'—to sell. Hair's too stiff. Maybe I can make me a cap out o' the big dark one. Sort o' like Dan'l Boone's cap, with the tail hangin' down."

"Gee, that would be fine," said Dan. "Ought to be good and warm. I wouldn't mind having one of those myself."

The three men were starting for the timber-lot. "Come along, boys," called the Judge. "We've got to hustle if we're goin' to git through by dinner-time."

They followed the lane up past the mowing-fields and into the pasture. At its farther edge a dark wall of woods rose against the sky. As they passed the clump of shagbark hickories half-way up the slope, Grandfather Garland stooped to pick up a handful of wind-fallen nuts. Dan watched him, fascinated, as he put one after another in his mouth and cracked their iron shells between his teeth.

"Great Henry!" Buckalew gasped. "Mean to say ye can do that at your age?"

"Humph!" chuckled the Judge. "Any time I can't

A TOUSLE-HEADED BOY OF ELEVEN

bust a pore little hick'ry nut, I'll know I *am* gittin' old!"

They opened the bars at the entrance to an old wood-road, and stepped into the cool shadow of the pines. It was quiet in the woods, and dark, except where filtered patches of sun came through to sprinkle the brown needle carpet with flecks of gold. A soft sound, like the *"hush-sh-sh . . . hush-sh-sh"* of waves on a beach, descended from the far green roof of the forest.

Buckalew stared about him and whistled. White pine everywhere. Clean, tall boles shooting upward, straight as ship-masts. Thousands of them, covering acre after acre.

Judge Garland smiled. "These are all right, for youngsters," he said. "The big ones are mostly over the other side o' the ridge."

"How big did ye say the lot was?" asked the mill-man.

"Just under three hundred acres," the Judge replied. "Tain't all like this, o' course. Some hardwood mixed in. I'd say about two hundred acres is solid cuttin' timber."

The wood-road curved upward toward a low knoll, half bare ledge and half sun-drenched grass and brambles. On the very top grew a monster pine-tree.

Its great roots went down into a cleft in the ledge. Its trunk, gnarled and massive, was a good six feet in diameter. A dozen feet above the ground it divided, and rose in twin columns, each a big tree in itself. It was ninety feet high. Not as tall as some of the younger pines they had seen, but gigantic in the spread of its green boughs.

For a moment the whole party stood in silence, looking up at the huge old tree.

Buckalew was the first to speak. "That one's been here a long time," he said thoughtfully. "Two hundred—maybe three hundred years."

"Shouldn't wonder," nodded the Judge. "Seems to me it's been as big as that ever since I can remember. Grandaddy of all the Garland pines—that old feller is."

Moving on across the ridge, they entered deep woods again on the farther slope. Here were pines to delight the heart of any lumberman. Many of them were thirty inches through at the butt, and loomed skyward a sheer hundred feet. Buckalew said little, but his keen eyes roved everywhere. Dan knew that he was doing mental arithmetic—estimating the cut —translating all that forest beauty into board feet.

At a fork in the woods-trail, Judge Garland stopped. "Guess I won't try to walk any further," he said. "You go right on, Ben, an' Jotham'll show you where the line fences run. I'll wait fer you up on the knoll."

Accompanied by the two boys, the old man retraced his steps to the ledge at the foot of the giant pine. Jack, the collie, raced here and there in the woods, returning every little while to make sure his master was still present.

The Judge took out his bandanna and wiped his rosy face. "Hot, here'n the sun," he smiled. "Feels good. Injun summer, I guess." Gently he stirred the pine needles with his walking-stick, and turned his head upward to look at the branching tree. "Yes," he said. "I shouldn't wonder if that chap was older'n the Pilgrim Fathers."

He pointed off to the southwest into the tall pines. "See that stand o' timber?" he asked. "Every bit o' that's grown from seed in seventy years. I can remember, plain as anything, when Uncle Eli had it cut over. I was a little shaver, smaller'n 'Lysses, here. There was no mill this side o' Riverdale, an' they took the logs out with oxen, workin' all one winter. I can see 'em now—two an' three yoke to a sled—haulin' down to the river.

"The choppers was goin' to cut this tree, too, but Uncle Eli wouldn't have it. I heard him tell Father, then, that if we left it here we'd have another growth o' pine. An' sure enough, we did. The rainy winds from the east blew down across this ridge an' carried the seed. First it was just stumps an' brush an' briers. Then the little green tops o' the pine seedlin's begun to show. When I was your age, Dan, we transplanted thousands of 'em. Took 'em from places where they'd started too thick, an' set 'em out over here on the pasture side."

He paused, ruminating, his eyes straying over the acres of woodland. "That's a long spell to wait," he said, "—a whole life-time. But we've got a good crop here, an' it's the second one I've lived to see!"

Dan watched him affectionately, sensing something of the old man's pride in the Garland pines.

"You're not going to let Buckalew cut this tree, are you, Grandpa?" he asked.

The Judge gave a snort. "I should say not!" he answered. "Seventy years from now, if you boys are still here, there'll be another fine stand o' pines right where these grew. Mark my words, an' remember what I'm tellin' ye."

He picked up a pine-cone, opening its spines to show them where the little brown seeds were housed. "Squirrels like to eat 'em," he said. "After the lot was cut over, Uncle Eli used to give me a penny for

HE POINTED OFF TO THE SOUTHWEST

every squirrel I killed, red or gray. Once I found a chipmunk's nest in a wall with half a peck o' pine seeds stored away. I took 'em and sowed 'em broadcast in the slashin'. Shouldn't wonder if some o' them very trees down yonder grew from what that chipmunk had gathered!"

At the end of half an hour they heard voices down the wood-road, and Buckalew reappeared with the farmer.

"Well, Ben," said the Judge, "did you git through it?"

The lumberman chewed a twig reflectively, and looked at the ground. In his own good time he nodded. "Best piece o' timber I ever cruised," he said. "Near as I can figger now, it'll cut better'n two an' a half million feet. All winter job, an' lucky if we git done by April."

"Not much to give any trouble, is there?" asked Judge Garland anxiously.

"No," replied Buckalew. "Clean as a whistle, right through. All that'll hold us back is the capacity o' the mill. Twenty thousand a day is good sawin'. We may hit a little higher average with this, because so much of it is clear butt sticks, good fer two-inch plank. Looks to me like less'n half of it'll run to box-boards."

"Fine!" grinned the Judge. "I kind o' thought you'd like the looks o' the job. How soon do we start?"

Buckalew glanced at him in surprise. "Hold on!" he said. "I ain't even told ye what it'll cost, yet."

"I don't aim to dicker about that," the old man winked. "Whatever you charge, it'll be robbery, so why fret over it?"

"Shucks!" said Buckalew. "That sort o' puts me on my honor to give ye a fair figger. I'll cut the whole thing for three-fifty a thousand. Five dollars if it's hauled an' loaded on the cars."

He looked up defiantly, as if still expecting an argument, but Judge Garland was holding out his hand.

"Done!" said he. "Five dollars loaded, it is. An' I only hope you make a little on the deal. Now tell me how quick we can expect the crew."

"Next week," the lumberman answered promptly. "We've finished, over in Maine. Ought to be set up an' ready to start sawin' by Friday. Where's the best water?"

They walked back along the wood-road to the pasture bars, and the Judge led the way down to the left. "How's this?" he asked.

A sizable brook flowed under the fence from the

next farm and cut across a corner of the pasture. Along its bank, on the side nearest the woods, was an acre or more of fairly level ground. The mill-man nodded his satisfaction.

"Couldn't be better," he said. "All right. I'll have to be movin' along now."

"No, ye don't!" expostulated the Judge. "It's noon, an' time to eat. Besides, that roan ought to be baited, if you expect him to stagger all the way home 'fore dark. Mrs. Grant's got places set fer all of us, unless I'm mistook."

His belief in that good lady's hospitality was justified. When they reached the yard she was standing in the kitchen door, waving to them with her apron.

"Dinner's on, folks," she called. "Come an' get it!"

It was a big table and a jolly one. There were three little Grant girls, all younger than 'Lysses, and—when they got over their first shyness—noisier.

It was when the meat and potatoes had been finished and they were all busy with apple pie and cheese, that Dan screwed up his courage to ask Mr. Buckalew an important question.

"Do you suppose," said he, flushing, "you could use me somehow around the mill, or in the woods?"

"Shouldn't wonder," nodded the lumberman. "There's 'most always a place for a spare hand. Can't pay very much, but ye'll learn a lot ye never knew before."

"Gee," said Dan, "that's sure good of you. I'll be ready to start next week then."

The Judge attempted a look of deep disgust. "Humph!" he growled. "Who'd have thought I'd ever raise my grandson to be a low-down lumberjack!"

But Dan could see he was mightily pleased, all the same.

III

IT BEGAN with a barking of dogs, far across the valley. First the distant baying of Mason's old hound, Ranger, a mile away to the eastward. Then the deep voice of Gillespie's big brindle terrier. Finally, nearer and more urgent, the yapping of half a dozen mongrel tykes, all the way from Dugan's crossing to the Garland gate.

Listening, as he raked leaves to cover the flower-beds, Dan wondered at the racket. It was nearly noon—a time when farm-dogs were ordinarily busy about their own affairs. Gradually another sound made itself heard. A measured clank and jingle, with a throbbing undercurrent of hoof-beats. A man's shout came faintly up the road, and a cracking noise like a pistol-shot.

Dan dropped his rake and ran toward the house. "Hey!" he yelled. "Debbie! Grandpa! I can hear 'em coming!"

Debbie hurried from the kitchen door, throwing a

shawl about her shoulders, and a moment later the Judge appeared.

"Where be they?" panted the old man eagerly. Dan pointed eastward along the valley road. A cloud of dust hung above the highway. In the middle of it, horses and men were moving, and a big, dark shape like a house swayed crazily.

"I'm going down to meet 'em," shouted Dan, and away he sped. A quarter of a mile down the road he met the vanguard of the procession. It was Buckalew, holding the roan down to a walk, and sitting sidewise on the buggy-seat to watch the cavalcade behind him. Four big horses strained at their collars as they pulled a heavy dray, loaded with machinery. Next came a double team with a full-fledged shanty— window, door, stovepipe and all—on wheels. And bringing up the rear was another four-horse hitch, hauling an iron boiler that looked like a miniature locomotive. The tall stack was folded down on hinges to keep it out of the way of overhanging limbs. A whole arsenal of lumberman's tools—axes, cant-hooks, cross-cut saws, shovels, lanterns and iron buck-ets—swung and jangled from a rack under the boiler.

Beside each of the three rigs plodded the drivers. They held their reins clustered in one hand and with the other swung their long-lashed whips, yelling hoarse encouragement to the sweating teams.

"Hup! G'long thar, Prince! Git on, Monk!" And above the shouts and the clatter of gear would come the whine and crack of the whirling blacksnakes.

It was an exciting spectacle—good as a circus parade, Dan told himself, as he walked alongside in the choking dust. The cruel noise of the whips made him shiver at first but he soon realized that the teamsters used them almost entirely as sound effects. Only once, when a wheeler was obviously shirking, did he see the lash flick out, light and sure, to send the horse into his collar again.

As the boy moved forward, past the first dray, he heard Buckalew call to him. "You're young Garland, ain't you?" asked the lumberman, peering through the dust. "Come on—hop in."

Dan climbed into the buggy. "We weren't looking for you till tomorrow," he said. "What time did you start?"

" 'Fore daybreak," Buckalew replied. "Got everythin' on the wagons last night, an' roused the teamsters out about three this mornin'. The rest o' the crew's comin' in Joe Whipple's buckboard. He's the sawyer."

There was a general halt as the procession came

abreast of the Garland house. The weary horses had a momentary rest while Buckalew talked with the Judge. Then the lumberman waved an arm and clucked to his roan. With a creak and a jangle the heavy loads lurched into motion once more.

Lunch was on the table when Dan went in. He ate hurriedly, then harnessed the mare and had her at the door when his grandfather came out. Babe smelled excitement and was eager to go. Just over the crest of the last rise they overtook the sawmill boiler. The little black whirled past, one wheel in the ditch, but she snorted and shied at a glimpse of the shanty rocking along ahead. It wasn't until they had turned in at the gate that she could be coaxed to go by.

Jotham Grant, grinning broadly, opened the bars to the pasture lane, and the motley parade went up the hill. In the level space beside the brook the steaming horses pulled to a stop. The sawyer's three-seater buckboard was there before them, and half a dozen men in lumberjacks' clothes were ready to go to work.

The first job was to put up a temporary camp. If Dan had wondered where the crew and horses would be quartered for the night, he soon found out. Buckalew issued a series of brisk orders and the men went into action. The drivers unhitched their teams, blanketed them and tied them along the fence. Four burly French Canadians took axes from the boiler wagon and started into the woods with one pair of horses. Whipple and another man drove lines of stakes to mark out the location of the mill and the camp buildings. Dan and 'Lysses and the dog, Jack, ran errands and tried to keep out from under foot.

Within an hour the choppers were back with a chain-load of stout hardwood saplings. Holes had been dug by the teamsters in the meantime, and even while the boys watched, a rough pole lean-to began to take shape. Boards, brought from the barn by Jotham Grant, were nailed across the top and down the sides in over-lapping rows, and the first shanty was finished.

"Here, Dan," Buckalew called. "Take a hay-rack up in the woods an' git us a load o' spruce boughs fer beds."

Accompanied by 'Lysses, Dan harnessed one of the Grant horses and set out. There was plenty of bushy young spruce along the line fence to the south, and in a few minutes the two boys had piled the rack high with fragrant branches. Back at the shanty, Whipple showed them how to lay them in springy rows, the butts pushed into the ground and the tips forming a soft, even upper surface.

A second pole shed was being thrown up by the men—a long, shallow lean-to which would serve as a stable for the horses. By supper-time the camp was ship-shape. A big cook-stove had been taken out of the wheeled shanty and set up in one end of the sleeping quarters. To an accompaniment of boisterous song, the cook stirred a huge kettle of stew. He was a squat, bald-headed man with hairy arms and a black patch over one eye that gave him a villainous look. Tim Gargan was his name, Dan learned. He was an old Alaskan sour-dough who had drifted east across Canada after the gold-rush, and had cooked in a score of camps in his day.

As the dark began to shut down, Judge Garland came looking for his grandson.

"Danny," he said, "I've fixed it up with the Grants fer you to board right here at the farm. We'll make out all right back home. That Frenchman down the road'll come in night and mornin' to do the chores. I had Debbie pack up some clothes an' brought 'em over this afternoon."

"Whee!" yelled 'Lysses. "Ain't that slick, Dan? You and me can sleep together, up in the garret."

"It's great," Dan replied. "Only—are you sure

you won't need me, down there? I hate like sin to think of any stranger working over Babe."

"I'll see that she gets fed an' groomed right," smiled the Judge. "An' how do you figger to earn your pay fer Buckalew if you ain't on hand to start work bright an' early in the mornin'?"

The old man climbed into the buggy and started home, while the two boys headed for the farm-house and supper.

Dan helped with the evening work at the barn, then made ready for bed. He had gathered from the talk of the men that tomorrow would be a big day, and he wanted to be on the job early. He and 'Lysses shared a wide old four-poster bed at the head of the attic stairs. Instead of springs, it had a bed-cord that creaked ominously at every motion. But the feather mattress was comfortable, and the boys slept soundly.

At daybreak Jotham Grant's voice hailed them forth. "Come on, you loafers," he called. "Rouse out o' that! I've milked six cows already, an' it's 'most the middle o' the mornin'."

The two youngsters pulled on their clothes and rushed downstairs. To Dan's relief the hour was only six-thirty by the alarm-clock in the kitchen. By seven he was up in the pasture, where he found the camp in full stir.

The choppers had cut and trimmed four heavy logs, to serve as a foundation for the mill. As soon as these were firmly in place the whole crew began the job of rolling the machinery off the dray. The huge circular saw and its base were bolted down to a frame of solid timbers. Then the long saw-carriage and track were set in place, with Whipple superintending every move. He had a rule in one hand and a spirit-level in the other.

"Watch him," one of the teamsters chuckled to Dan. "Fussy as an old woman about the way that saw sets. He shore knows what he's doin', though. Wait till ye see him make her hum, when the cuttin' starts!"

A compact two-cylinder steam engine was the next thing to be moved. Dan saw that though it was far from new, every moving part was clean and freshly oiled, and even the cylinder-head nuts were brightly polished. They bolted the engine-bed down to the solid timbers just behind the saw-carriage, its heavy drive-wheel lined up with the pulley on the shaft of the saw.

The boiler was wheeled into position between the engine and the brook. Immediately the fireman set about connecting his steam pipes and running a length of thick hose from the boiler down into the stream. He was a tall, middle-aged Swede, slow of speech but good-humored and a hard worker. The men called him Ole.

The rest of the crew, meanwhile, were taking the bark off two straight forty-foot logs and trimming one side so that they would lie flat on the ground. These were the "skids." They were laid side by side about ten feet apart, the lower ends only a few inches from the saw-carriage. Dan had seen mills in operation before, and knew that the fresh-cut logs would be piled along the skids, ready to be rolled on to the carriage.

Buckalew came over to where the boy was standing. "She's beginnin' to look like a mill," he said. "Prob'ly seems all sort o' mixed up to you, but ye'll see how it works in a day or two. I won't bother to introduce ye 'round to all the men, but I'll tell ye now, so ye'll understand when I give ye a job with any of 'em.

"Whipple is boss around the mill. Next to him is the marker. He ain't here yet but ye'll know him by his havin' only one arm. Frenchman, name o' 'Poleon Duval. He's stronger an' quicker with that one hand than most men are with two.

"Mel Rollins, workin' there on the skids, is the

roller-on, an' Bill Bean is the pit-man. That's Bill—
the lanky feller helpin' mount the slab-saw. Ole Jenson fires the boiler, an' that makes the last o' the
mill-crew.

"In the woods there's two head choppers—Pete
Brosseau an' Leo Duquette. Each of 'em has a helper

an' a swamper. All French Canucks. They make the
best ax-men, if they're kept away from liquor.

"The teamsters sort o' run themselves. Johnny
Couture an' Red Nolan do the reg'lar drivin' fer us,
an' take care o' the blacksmith work. Both good men
with horses. Well, that's the whole gang, outside o'
the cook an' myself. A tight little outfit, but powerful
fast on its feet. Once we git steam up, ye'll see some
hustlin'."

Up the hill in the thick timber Dan could hear the
ring of axes. The choppers and swampers had left

the mill-crew to finish setting up the machinery and were already at work in the woods. Soon the red-haired teamster, Nolan, threw the harness on his big bays and hitched them to a "scoot"—a stoutly built sled with wooden runners. No wagons were used in the woods-hauling. The stumps and roots and brush would have smashed a wheel to bits in a few hours. Instead, summer or winter, the logs were snaked out to the mill on scoots.

"Ye might go ahead in with the team," said Bucka-lew, "an' see how it's done."

Nolan, striding along beside the home-made sled, turned a frank Irish grin on Dan as he came up.

"Hi, kid," he said affably. "Goin' to be a lumber-jack? That's the stuff! Only git this in yer head furrst. It's the horrses an' the drivers that keeps the mill a-goin'. Wan good teamster is worth three choppers. An' don't let any Frenchie tell ye different!"

He ended with a chuckle and whistled a jig as he marched along. They entered the old wood-road, and in a hundred yards or so they reached the scene of the first cutting operations. Burly Pete Brosseau and his helper had scarfed a good-sized tree, close to the track, and were plying the two-man saw. Back and forth the steel sped with a steady *zing—zing—zing* that was like a kind of fierce music.

Nolan halted the team and glanced at the deep-bitten scarf in the base of the pine. "They're fallin' her over that way," he pointed. "We're all right, here."

The shrill song of the saw-blade came to an abrupt finish. Dan saw the two Frenchmen straighten up, looking intently aloft.

"Comin' down!" yelled Brosseau. There was a single cracking sound in the tree trunk, a gentle swaying of the top, as if a gust of wind had caught it. Then the stricken tree gathered momentum and surged earthward with a rending roar that shook the forest.

The crash was followed by a rustle of falling leaves and twigs. Brosseau waved cheerfully at Nolan.

"Pretty good, eh?" he called. "Missed dat leetle spruce by t'ree inch'—jus' lak I tell her to!"

The teamster spat disparagingly. "Thought I'd find a load o' logs," he addressed Dan. "An' here they're only gittin' the furrst one down. Guess you won't see the mill worrkin' 'fore tomorrer."

"Hi!" shouted the Frenchman, springing into action. "Cantillon—Louis—breeng dose ax'!"

"That got him," Nolan laughed under his breath. "Watch 'em go, now!"

Brosseau's helper, Louis Bergeron, ran along the

THE STRICKEN TREE SURGED EARTHWARD

tree, ax in hand. As he reached the first limbs his blade began to swing. And at every stroke a pine branch fell, lopped off cleanly at the trunk. A big young Frenchman came out of the woods to the left, and joined him. It was the swamper, Cantillon. Brosseau himself was measuring off the cuts. Four lengths of his ax and then a deep notch through the bark— four more lengths and another notch. There were six of these twelve-foot cut-marks between the butt and the tapering top.

The trimming finished, Bergeron darted back like a cat along the trunk. He took one end of the crosscut saw, Brosseau the other, and without a word they set its teeth in the first mark.

Fascinated, Dan watched them go to work. Their motions were swift, graceful, apparently effortless. Standing with legs wide, knees bent springily, they swung from the hips in a sure, smooth pull that made the saw bite deep at every stroke. A stream of fragrant white sawdust shot from either side of the cut. In an unbelievably short time the big butt-log was severed from the trunk, and with hardly a pause the two men moved on to the next mark.

At the other end of the tree, meanwhile, Cantillon was chopping steadily. His ax strokes were quick and true. The slim top-log was already cut through,

and he finished the second almost as soon as the men
with the saw. As they went to work on the last re-
maining cut, he laid down the ax, picked up a cant-
hook and began rolling the logs to the edge of the
road.

"Not bad, boys," said Nolan grudgingly. "Keep
that up all winter, an' us teamsters won't have time
fer our afternoon naps!"

He gathered the reins and guided the bays deftly
forward among the trees. The scoot was turned and
brought up alongside the first log. Dan picked up a
peavy and started to help load, but Nolan waved
him back. "Watch how it's done, first, or ye'll be
strainin' yerself," he grinned.

The peavy, or cant-hook, is an implement almost
as important in lumbering as an ax. It has a stout
four-foot handle with a steel spike at the end, and
a steel hook hinged to its under-side. With it, one
or two men can move a big log with ease.

There was hardly any lifting, the boy realized, as
Cantillon and the teamster rolled the logs up on the
sled. Just a matter of leverage and timing. Almost
before he knew it, the six lengths of pine were loaded,
and a long chain slung over them to keep them on.

"Hup!" yelled Nolan. "Gi' up there, Duke!" The

bays settled their feet and bowed forward like one horse.

"Here we go, kid," the Irishman called to Dan. "Ye'll have to hustle to keep up with this pair!"

A cheer greeted them from the mill as they came out of the woods.

"First load!" shouted the sawyer. "Ole, got that steam up yet?"

And with a thrill of excitement Dan saw that smoke was coming from the boiler stack.

IV

WHEN Dan had helped roll the logs off the sled onto the skids, he had time to look around him. The men had been working methodically all morning. Over the saw and the carriage stood the frame-work of a long shed, raised on half a dozen stout posts. There was no roof as yet, but the structure began to look like a real sawmill.

It took time to get a head of steam on the wood-burning boiler. Ole had collected a pile of dry sticks and branches with which he was now feeding a roaring blaze. Every minute or two the fire-door would clang open, to swallow another armful of fuel.

"Askin' is steam up yet!" exclaimed the Swede. "Ay bane lucky if Ay got 'nough steam to blow whistle when it comes twelve o'clock!"

He fished a cheap watch out of his overalls-pocket by a braided leather thong. "By Viminy, it's eatin' time, now!" he said, reaching for the whistle-cord. A long, shrill hoot woke the pasture echoes and sent Grant's cows into a frightened huddle. The choppers and swampers began straggling out of the woods, and the mill-crew laid down their tools. Dan, starting for the farm-house, was stopped by a sound of argument down beside the brook.

"What's the matter with me?" a truculent voice was saying. "Ain't I good enough to work with yer dirty Canucks?"

Looking around the end of the boiler, the boy saw Buckalew facing a big, raw-boned youth in a ragged sweater. The lumberman's reply was too low-pitched for Dan to hear, but there was finality in the jerk of his thumb toward the gate. The lanky intruder's face darkened.

"Yeah?" he growled. "Maybe I'll be back, an' when I do you'll have a job fer me."

He swung away and went shambling down the lane. Dan, going in the same direction, was only a score of paces behind him when young 'Lysses and his dog appeared in the barn-yard. The collie started racing toward Dan and stopped, in passing, to sniff at the stranger's legs.

With an ugly oath, the fellow drew back his foot and launched a kick that caught the dog in the ribs. Jack's quick yelp of pain changed to a growl, and he would have been at the stranger's throat if 'Lysses had not seized him by the collar.

"Don't try that again!" the boy blazed fiercely. "I'll let him take a piece out o' your hide next time!"

When the unwelcome visitor had gone off down the road, the two boys went toward the kitchen. "Who was he, do you know?" asked Dan.

"Sure," said 'Lysses. "A low-down skunk named Daggett. Used to live a mile or so above here. Oh, Paw—" he called, as his father came out of the barn, "—how come Ike Daggett is round here? I thought they put him in jail."

Jotham Grant looked disturbed. "Was that him?" he frowned. "He got six months fer stealin' chickens. Sorry he's come back to this neighborhood, now he's out. Have to lock things up more careful, I guess."

The noon meal was over, 'Lysses started back to

school and Dan returned to the mill. The men had finished eating and were lighting their pipes. Buckalew went down to the boiler, looked at the steam-gauge, and spoke to Ole.

"Come on, boys," he called. "Git these logs sawed. If we don't have some buildin's up before the first freeze comes, you're goin' to sleep cold."

The mill-crew went to their stations and the fireman turned the steam-valve. With a grunt and a wheeze, the pistons began to move. The sawyer bent above the engine lovingly, oil-can in hand, then let in the clutch to set the huge saw spinning. By the time Mel Rollins had rolled the first log on the carriage and jerked down the clamps, everything was running smoothly. The carriage rumbled into motion and the saw-teeth sank into the end of the log with a high-pitched whine. Dan felt like cheering as he saw the first slab fall away. The big job was started at last. He watched that butt-log turned into two-by-sixes and two-by-fours—frame lumber for the bunkhouse, Whipple told him. Then, as the second stick was rolled on, Red Nolan called him for another trip with the team.

All afternoon Dan worked—really worked—in the woods. Under Nolan's direction he made progress in the art of using a peavy, learned the trick of setting the swinging jaw in the bark and lifting with his shoulder under the end of the handle. "Getting his weight into it," the red-haired teamster called it. By night there were blisters on his palms but he had helped load and unload the scoot half a dozen times. A good-sized pile of sweet-smelling new lumber stood by the mill when dusk fell. And in the morning all hands turned to the erection of buildings to house them for the winter.

The bunk-house was a low, single-room structure, forty feet long by twenty wide. It had four windows and two doors and over the rough-sawn boards, it was roofed and sheathed with tar-paper. Most of the men were fairly good carpenters at a pinch, and they had the building finished in two working days. Inside, it was spacious enough to accommodate a board table and benches down the middle, sixteen bunks along the walls, a cook-stove and utensils at one end and a round-bellied heater at the other. A sort of shed, built onto the kitchen-end, served as a store-room for provisions.

The teamsters, with Dan to help them, were busy meanwhile on a job of their own. They rebuilt the temporary stable lean-to that had been thrown up the first day—giving it a front wall and a door, as well as one window. The boy enjoyed this job, for he

ALL AFTERNOON DAN WORKED

found he was handier with a hammer and hand-saw than either of the drivers. Any time Nolan and Johnny Couture were together there was entertainment worth listening to. Johnny was a stout, happy-go-lucky French Canadian with a quaint turn of speech and a way with horses. He was no match for the sharp-tongued Irishman in repartee, but he seemed to relish their arguments nevertheless.

"Dose hoss' o' Red's," he told Danny, "dey're prett' good wan, if dey was han'le right. Duke, she's tough hoss. Come from Canada, dat's why. Pull lak a son-of-a-gun, a'right. Prince, she's good 'nough hoss, too —if dat Irish fella knows how for mak' him work. Some tam Red gits sick an' I drive 'em, me. Den you see."

"Don't count on it, Frenchie," said Nolan. "I'll be almighty careful to stay well, if that's yer plan. Sure, an' I don't blame ye fer wantin' to git yer hands on a real pair fer once, though. Them skinny goats o' yourn must be terrible disappointin' to drive."

As a matter of fact, Dan was impressed by both teams. Nolan's big bays were sturdily built, strong and willing. Prince was a young Western horse—one of the thousands that are shipped to New England from Iowa and Illinois each year for farm and woods work. Duke, on the other hand, was of that tough breed known as a Canada "chunk." Square-rumped, close-coupled and sure-footed, he was as much at home in the winter woods as a moose.

Johnny Couture called his black pair Monk and Ginger. They must have weighed a good two hundred pounds less than the bays. Quick-stepping, wiry horses, so perfectly matched that the evener hardly wavered an inch when they were pulling. Johnny grained them well but what they ate went into nervous energy instead of into weight.

"Never mind, Frenchie," Dan heard Nolan tell their driver. "You're fat enough to make up fer the pore beasts!"

That week-end the boy went home to spend Saturday night and Sunday. To his relief, everything was going smoothly there. Babe was as sleek as a kitten, and old Judy's bedding was clean and fresh. Dan finished the morning chores on Sunday, got into his good suit and drove the Judge and Debbie to church. It was when they were returning, at noon, that he saw a lanky figure in a tattered sweater waiting for them on the steps. It was Ike Daggett. Coming back from the barn, Dan found the fellow talking to his grandfather in the office. They stayed closeted there for some time, and when Daggett departed, the old gentleman's face was grave.

He picked up his paper and sat down heavily in the old arm-chair by the window.

"Worthless cuss," he remarked. "But I don't want to be uncharitable. Pretty hard, I guess, fer a feller that's been in jail to git a job. I knew the boy's mother. Widow-woman. Worked her fingers raw to keep a home fer Ike an' send him to school. Guess her heart would be broke if she'd lived to see him like he is now."

When Monday morning came, Dan rose before daybreak, got the work done, and was ready by seven o'clock to start for the timber-lot. His grandfather was silent during most of the drive. When they reached Grant's yard, the Judge tied Babe to the fence and went to talk to Buckalew.

"Goin' to ask you quite a favor, Ben," he said. "I understand you've got a full crew an' don't really need a spare hand. Still, this boy Daggett's got to be took care of somehow or he'll go back to stealin'. He's big and strong enough. Ought to be smart in the woods, too. If you'll give him a trial, I'm willin' to pay half his wages, fer his ma's sake."

The lumberman looked at the ground. "Don't like to do it, Judge," he answered. "He's no good. Come up here half-drunk, Friday, an' started to git tough. You know I won't stand liquor around the job. If I put him on, it'll be my own responsibility, an' I'll pay the wages. But if he makes one slip, he's done. I'll go with ye, that far."

"Thanks," said the Judge. "Guess I couldn't ask anythin' fairer'n that. He'll be up to see you to-morrow."

As soon as the bunk-house and stable were completed, work in the woods began in earnest. The weather held clear and bright, and though they had a heavy frost each morning, it was warm enough by mid-day to shed jackets and sweaters.

"The job where ye can be most help right now," Buckalew told Dan, "is out with the swampers. We've got to have our roads cleared before snow flies, so's the choppers an' teamsters can keep up with the mill. Git yer ax ground an' go 'long with Fleury an' Cantillon today."

The two young Frenchmen were congenial company. Dan found them as simple and unassuming as children. Both had been raised in Quebec Province, and this was only their second winter in the States. Cantillon, big and dark and powerful, was looking forward to the day when he would be a head chopper at three dollars a day, and could bring his girl from Canada. He talked about her a good deal and sang sentimental French ditties in a rolling bass. Her name, Dan learned, was Marie-Josephine, and she tended geese on a farm somewhere near Three Rivers.

Raoul Fleury was smaller in build and had ruddy blond hair and blue eyes. He was a merry youth, also given to singing in the woods. But his tunes were quaint old voyageur songs, and he was too much interested in girls in general to moon over any single love.

They knew their business. In order to keep a balance in the length of the hauls, it would be necessary to have one crew of choppers start at the far side of the lot, while the other worked nearer home. Roads had to be cut and brush cleared in advance, and this was their job, for the present.

With canny judgment, Raoul would ferret out a path through the trees, blazing the way with his ax. His practiced eye knew at a glance which way the choppers would want to fall the big ones, and he kept his road out of reach of the descending tops. Behind him came Cantillon and Dan, cutting a track from six to eight feet wide, with as few sharp turns as possible. Each sapling they took out was chopped close to the ground. They tried to leave no sharp stubs that would bother the horses or catch the cross-braces of the scoot.

Dan had always thought himself a pretty good

ax-man. But he was far from being a match for Cantillon. It amazed him to see the big Canadian take his easy swing at a young hemlock, thick as his arm, and shear it off cleanly at the roots.

At the end of a week they had finished three tracks that radiated from the pasture bars to the outer edge of the pines. The choppers, meanwhile, had been cutting steadily, and the sawing was in full swing. Between the stable and the woods, neat stacks of pine lumber had begun to rise.

"Made close to a hundred thousand foot this week," said Buckalew when the work stopped, Saturday afternoon. "Pretty fair fer a start, but we can do better when we're really into it. A little snow'll be a help—make faster haulin'."

Ike Daggett had made his appearance on Tuesday and was put to work "sticking" lumber. His job was to take the new-sawn boards as they were hauled from the pit and stack them up in piles to dry, with strips of edging laid between each two tiers of lumber. He was regarded tolerantly enough by the other men, though none of them had much to say to him.

Dan, returning to Green Hill on Saturday night, found the Judge anxious to hear how his protegé was doing.

"Oh, he's making out all right," the boy answered

him. "He sleeps in the bunk-house with the rest, and seems to do his work. I heard Ben Buckalew say he guessed Ike had earned his money. Some o' the boys told me they'd be careful to hide their pay under the pillow, but I don't think they're really worried. Maybe he's trying to go straight, and if he behaves himself they won't give him any trouble."

"I'm glad to hear that," nodded the Judge with relief. "He might amount to somethin' after all, an' I was bound to give him the chance."

Dan started to tell his grandfather about Daggett's brutal treatment of the collie at Grant's, but thought better of it. There was no reason to disturb the old man's peace of mind. Perhaps it was whisky that had made the ex-convict ugly that day.

"I reckon when a chap's been in trouble," he thought as he lay in bed that night, "the squarest thing is to let him work it out for himself."

But on Monday, when he got back to the job, he was glad his grandfather had left without talking to Buckalew. There was a grim look in the lumberman's eyes when he encountered Dan.

"Seen anything o' Daggett?" he asked. "He ain't shown up today, an' Bill Bean says he was in Roach's saloon down to Riverdale, Saturday night. Looks to me like trouble."

V

By noon, that first Monday of November, there was a gray haze over the sun, and the air felt heavy and cold. Dan's blue flannel shirt and mackinaw barely served to keep out the leaden chill. In the woods he noticed the ominous stillness of the pines, and worked in a gloom that was almost like twilight.

"Storm, she's come sure," said Johnny Couture. "Mebbe tonight—mebbe tomorrow, we git some snow. You see."

The horses were restless, shaking themselves with a jingle of trace-chains, and blowing clouds of steam through their nostrils. The men worked with one eye on the weather but fast and steadily, as if anxious to get a given amount done before the snow started. Down at the mill the sawing went on without interruption. Jotham Grant was taking Daggett's place at the sticking. Most of his autumn work was out of the way, and he was glad of a chance to earn some extra money.

Dan helped him as usual with the evening chores,

gave 'Lysses a hand with his home-work and was ready for bed by nine. Long after the youngster beside him had fallen asleep, he lay there huddled under the quilts, listening to a rising wind that came moaning out of the hills. It sniffed and whined in the chimney top like a stealthy animal. It rattled at the windows and searched the crevices around the eaves. At last he heard a softer sound—a muffled whisper of whirling flakes. It had begun to snow. Dan turned over comfortably and went to sleep.

The storm was over at daybreak, and a pink sunrise glistened on miles of white fields and snow-frosted woods. Only a couple of inches had fallen, but it served to lighten the pulling for the teams and seemed to lift the spirits of the camp. Ole Jenson was quavering some kind of Scandinavian folk-song as he worked the hand-pump that filled the boiler. Red Nolan came out of the stable with a curry-comb in his hand and danced a jig in the new snow. It was lumbering weather.

Everybody worked with a will that day, and Dan was not surprised to hear, when he came in with the last load at sundown, that the marker's tally-sheet showed twenty-two thousand feet—the best record they had made. He met Jotham Grant down by the barn. "Well," said the farmer, "did ye see Daggett?"

"No," Dan replied. "Is he back?"

"Yep. Come in this afternoon. Gave Buckalew a story about bein' took sick, Sunday. Said he couldn't git out o' bed 'thout faintin' spells, till today. I don't reckon Ben liked it, but he let him go to work. The feller did look sort o' shaky. He might be tellin' the truth, at that."

When the milking was done and supper eaten, Dan pulled a chair into the circle around the lamp. He had a new copy of the *Youth's Companion,* and was deep in a hunting story by C. A. Stephens. After a while 'Lysses yawned and slammed his geography book shut.

" 'Night," he said. "I'm goin' to bed." As he passed the window by the foot of the stairs he stopped suddenly.

"Listen," he whispered. "What was that?"

For a moment Dan heard nothing. Then there came a faint crash and a noise of distant shouting.

"Sounded as if it came from the mill," said Dan. "You'd better stay here, 'Lysses. I'm going up there an' see what's happening."

He snatched his cap and mackinaw from their peg in the shed and went out across the snowy yard. Intermittently the sounds continued to reach him—not singing or laughter but a confused clamor of angry voices. He went up the lane at a run and pulled up panting in front of the bunk-house.

The door was open. Inside, in the yellow haze of lantern-light, he could see men's bodies moving swiftly. There was another crash as someone fell to the floor. Big Pete Brosseau stood by an overturned bench, stripped to the waist, and beat his hairy chest with both fists.

"Come on, you!" he yelled belligerently. "I show you who's goin' be boss, 'roun' here. I'm de bes' fightin' man in camp, me!"

There was a babel of derisive howls and another man flung himself on the burly chopper. But just at that instant Dan was pushed out of the way and Ben Buckalew strode into the whirlwind of flying fists.

The gray-haired lumberman jerked the knot of combatants apart with powerful hands and uttered a short, sharp command.

"Stop it!"

The hush was instant. Two of the men picked themselves hastily off the floor. Brosseau leaned against the table, chest heaving, eyes staring glassily at his employer.

"Where's the liquor?" asked Buckalew harshly.

There was a movement of eyes toward one of the

bunks. The mill-man walked over to it and lifted out a half-empty gallon jug of whisky.

"Whose bunk is this?"

"Daggett's," someone muttered.

"You, Daggett—" snapped Buckalew, "—git yer things together."

Sullenly the fellow complied, gathering up an untidy bundle of his spare clothes. Buckalew meanwhile went over to the door and poured the whisky out in the snow. Then he took hold of Daggett's shoulder and propelled him across the threshold. "Start movin'," he said, "an' don't stop this side o' the main road. I don't want to see ye 'round here again."

Daggett's old skating-cap of red knitted wool had fallen to the floor. Buckalew picked it up and slapped it on the trouble-maker's head, then gave him a final shove. Daggett stumbled on for half a dozen yards before he turned to snarl a phrase over his shoulder.

"Maybe ye won't —*see* me—" were the words Dan caught. Then Buckalew's voice cut in sharply. "I said don't stop!" he snapped, and Daggett moved on.

"Git to bed, you boys," ordered the lumberman, facing the crowd in the bunk-house. Then without a further glance he stalked off toward the wheeled shanty where he had his own quarters.

Dan saw the door close after him and went down

the lane to the farm-house. In the starlight the distant shape of Ike Daggett showed dark against the snow —a tall, hunched figure, plodding away along the road.

It took the boy a while to get to sleep that night. The excitement of that roaring, drunken fight in the bunk-house was still tingling in his veins. He thought he had known the crew so well—a gay gang, but good-natured, hard-working, keen-witted. The glimpse of Brosseau's distorted face and berserk fists had shown him a totally different side of lumber-camp life.

In the morning the whole incident appeared to be forgotten. Around the mill there was the usual cheerful bustle, and though Dan saw one or two of the men looking a bit sheepish when Buckalew passed, the lumberman was as coolly matter-of-fact as ever.

Only when the woods-crews were starting out did he show signs of irritation. "You're a man short," he said. "Where's Pete?"

The Frenchmen shook their heads and looked uncomfortable. "She's go 'way," mumbled Louis Bergeron finally. "Las' night she's go off to git drunk."

"Great thunderin' guns!" Buckalew exploded. "Has it started this quick? I should ha' knocked that fool's head off, when he first showed up, pesterin' me fer a job!"

He turned to Dan. "You can tell your Gran'pop that's what comes o' bein' soft-hearted," he said bitterly. "I can't even go an' fetch Brosseau back, or we'll be left short-handed. Reckon Johnny Couture'll have to turn chopper today, an' I'll drive his team."

Dan's face reddened. "Maybe I could handle the team," he answered. "Or, listen—let me go after Pete. I can bring him back."

Buckalew looked at him, considering. "All right. Try it," said he. "Ye can take my hoss an' buggy. Guess ye'll find him in one o' the bars, at Riverdale."

The mill-man's big roan trotter, Major, was no easy horse to harness. He had been short of exercise the past week, and the cold morning air worked on his pent-up energies. Dan finally had to tie his head to a corner of the stable and pull the buggy up behind him to get him into the shafts. Then they were off.

The light snow had been firmly packed by a day's hauling, and the wheels sang on the crisp surface. Dan had to fight the big horse at first to keep him from bolting. Then, when they were out on the road and clear of fences, he gave him his head. As soon as he felt the reins slacken, Major settled down to business. He had only one idea and that was to travel like the wind—up hill, down hill and around curves.

A TALL, HUNCHED FIGURE

Driving this four-legged steam-engine was very different, Dan found, from holding the lines over a smooth-gaited trotter like Babe. The roan racked the buggy at every stride. He had a tremendous reach, and his big hoofs fell with a solid smack. When they crossed a wooden bridge the sound was like a sudden cannonade.

At the end of three or four miles the horse was dark with sweat. Dan soothed him by voice and steadied him with the lines. Finally he succeeded in reducing the furious pace to a reasonable road-speed. It was nine good miles to Riverdale. But as they jogged down the last hill into the town, the boy looked at his watch and found they had covered the distance in forty minutes.

Down North Main Street he drove, and through the upper square. It was the middle of the morning and most of the hitching-places were occupied, but he found a vacant space at last, and tied and blanketed the roan.

Dan didn't know much about saloons but they were not hard to locate. There were swinging doors on most of the prominent corners. He started with the Rollins House Bar and made the rounds. At that hour there were few customers on hand. In each place he visited, two or three habitual topers would stare at him, watery-eyed, and the bar-tender would stop polishing glasses to give him a hostile glance. No, they hadn't seen anybody by the name of Brosseau. No, they had a high-class place, and didn't go for the lumber-camp trade.

By the time Dan had searched all the bars on Main Street it was nearly noon. He went into a dairy lunch down near the railroad station and had a sandwich and a glass of milk. As he sat on his high stool at the counter his view commanded a narrow side alley across the way. Suddenly a door in the alley opened, and a big man was pushed violently out. He lurched against the opposite wall, then his knees sagged and he went down limply, like a sack of grain.

Dan gulped his milk and hurried out. The building behind which the man lay showed a window with dingy lettering—"Mike Roach's Saloon." Of course! He'd heard that name before. Running over to the prostrate figure he raised one heavy shoulder and looked at the face. It was Pete Brosseau—hopelessly drunk.

Here was a dilemma. Dan was strong but he knew he could never carry that dead weight out to the buggy. And he didn't like to leave him there, for fear a passing policeman might see him. Riverdale didn't countenance drunks lying in the gutter.

He opened the rear door of the saloon and went in. A few noisy freight-handlers from the railroad yards were drinking at the smelly tables. A thick-set Irishman in shirt-sleeves and apron came into the backroom from the bar and scowled at Dan.

"Phwat ye doin' in here, b'y?" he demanded.

"That French lumberjack you just threw out," said Dan, "—I want to take him back to camp. But I can't get him into the buggy without some help."

"Phere's your rig?" growled the saloon-keeper.

"Up at the square. It won't take long to bring it here, though."

"Go git it," Roach replied. "I'll fix him."

Dan sped up the street and returned in a moment with the horse and buggy. The Irishman had Brosseau on his feet and was holding him up with one powerful hand gripped in the lapels of his jacket. With the other he now proceeded to slap the big chopper's face—once—twice—methodically and hard.

Brosseau gasped and looked about him with a wild stare. "What—who—" he choked— "C'm' on! I can lick de whole bunch, me!"

"That's right, Frenchie! Sure ye can," Roach agreed, patting his shoulder. "We're goin' to take ye there right now, so ye can show thim!"

He half pushed, half lifted the aroused woodsman

into the buggy-seat and pulled the robe around his knees.

"There y' are, kid," he muttered to Dan. "He'll go to sleep again in a minute. Watch he don't fall out."

The boy turned Major around and headed for camp once more. By his side Brosseau sat slumped low, a warm bulk that reeked of spirits. Occasionally he would wave his arm in a gesture of scorn, or mumble a few pugnacious phrases. But 'by the time they had climbed the hill and were clear of the town, he was snoring heavily again. The boy made sure the robe was tucked securely under him to hold him in, and then touched the roan with the whip.

The big horse had passed his first enthusiasm, but he was willing to travel. They rocked along at a good pace and reached the Grant farm a little after one. Jotham was up in the pasture sticking lumber. At Dan's hail, the farmer's wife came out of the kitchen.

"My good lands!" she exclaimed. "What you got there? He ain't dead, is he?"

"No," said Dan, "not quite, but I'll need some help getting him sobered up. Wait a second."

He seized the Frenchman's shoulders and shook him awake. "Come on, Pete," he said. "You're home now. Time to get out."

Between them, Dan and Mrs. Grant hauled the big man to the ground and set him on uncertain legs. There was a wooden pump and a horse trough in the yard, beside the barn, and toward it they led him.

"Pretty hot, isn't it, Pete?" said the boy cheerfully. "Let's take off our jackets." The chopper made no objection to being relieved of his mackinaw, and even his flannel shirt. The next part of Dan's plan took some maneuvering. He steered his unwieldy charge up to the trough, and signaled Mrs. Grant to man the pump-handle. Then he skipped around to the opposite side.

"Here, Pete—how about a drink?" he urged, holding the tin dipper just out of the Frenchman's reach. As Brosseau swayed forward, the boy caught his arm and pulled him downward. In a jiffy the big chopper was sprawled across the trough, face down, his naked back directly under the spout. Dan gripped his neck with both hands and held him there securely.

"Now pump!" he yelled. "Quick and plenty!"

A torrent of icy water splashed over the luckless Pete. As Mrs. Grant's stout arms flew up and down the stream increased in volume. And it was so cold that Dan's hands were numb where it poured over them.

A startled snort came from Brosseau. Then a

spluttering howl of anguish. He waved his arms frantically and his knees beat a tattoo on the side of the trough, but still Dan kept him down. After perhaps fifteen seconds of this heroic treatment, the boy released his grasp and Mrs. Grant stopped pumping. The big chopper's frame shook with a convulsive shiver. Groping with his hands he found the edge of the trough and reared himself erect.

"I k-k-keel you!" he gasped, through chattering teeth. And with an awkward lunge he made for Dan. Tantalizingly the boy skipped out of the way. He snatched up Brosseau's shirt and jacket and started up the lane at a run—the Frenchman pounding at his heels.

"Take care o' the horse!" Dan yelled to the farmer's wife. "I'll be back!"

It was a long three hundred yards from the barnyard to the door of the bunk-house. Dan ran easily, glancing back from time to time to make sure he was not too far in the lead. Brosseau was panting hoarsely before he reached the pasture, but he stuck to the chase. Dan slowed almost to a walk at the end. The stocky woodsman came after him on staggering legs, his mouth gaping wide in a struggle for air. He stumbled across the doorstep and sank exhausted on a bench while the boy dodged around the table. Dan's own breath was short, but more from laughter than from the run.

"Listen, Pete," he said. "Don't get so sore. I had to do that. You were drunk, Pete—ossified! You know what those other choppers were saying? They said nobody'd miss Pete Brosseau in the woods anyway. Leo Duquette claims his crew can keep the mill going without you!"

Comprehension dawned in the Frenchman's eyes. *"Diable!"* he gurgled. "Dose bum says I'm no-good chopper—me?"

"Sure!" Dan answered. "I knew you'd want to show 'em. That's why I went after you—and gave you that bath. How do you feel now?"

Brosseau stood up. He was still a bit shaky on his feet, but there was a grim purpose in the set of his black brows. "By gar!" he growled. "I don' feel so good, but I kin chop plenty for show dose Duquette gang! Gimme my shirt!"

VI

TIM GARGAN appeared from behind the cook-stove in time to hear the big chopper's words. He had been peeling potatoes and still had the kitchen-knife in his hand.

"Attaboy, Pete!" he grinned. "I bet you kin cut more timber 'fore dark than Leo's got down all day. Here—lemme help ye button that shirt."

Over the Frenchman's shoulder he winked at Dan with his one good eye. When the dressing operation was complete he handed Brosseau his ax and went with them to the door.

"Slick job, Danny," he murmured in the boy's ear. "You handled him about perfect."

There was only a single log left on the skids when they went past the mill. Mel Rollins leaned on his peavy and stared.

" 'Bout time you was back, Pete," he called. "We'll be sawin' air here in a minute."

"By gar!" shouted Brosseau. "I sen' you down some sawin' pretty queek!"

At the entrance to the wood-road they met a team
—Johnny Couture's blacks—with Buckalew driving.
The scoot was loaded light, with two small logs under
the chain.

The mill-man caught sight of Dan and Brosseau,
and pulled the horses to a sudden stop.

"Well, I'll be—" he ejaculated. For a moment
he looked as if he were about to laugh. Then he bent
a stern frown on the chopper. "Look here, Pete," he
said, "how sober are you? I don't want any feet cut
off, or trees comin' down on folks' heads."

"Me, I'm a'right now, Boss," answered the shame-
faced Frenchman. "You wanna watch me? I show
you some choppin'!"

"Go ahead," said Buckalew. "Couture's tryin' to
do your job, an' makin' a poor fist of it. Send him
down to the mill fer the team."

They found Pete's crew sweating away at a big
pine in the nearest cutting. Johnny Couture let go
of his end of the saw and stood up wearily, wiping
his round face.

"Git out, you hoss-driver," snorted Brosseau, "an'
let a lumberjack work!"

He spit in his palms and seized the saw handle.
And Bergeron, grinning on the other side of the tree,
caught hold with a will. Dan had never seen a cross-

cut blade fly so fast. Big Pete's face was gray and beads of perspiration stood on his brow, but he never let up in his sawing till the pine came down.

That tree and five more like it fell before Brosseau's furious attack that afternoon. By dusk he was so spent that Dan had to help him out of the woods, and he was violently sick on the way. When it was over he grinned wanly. "I been feelin' dat way, right 'long," he croaked. "But I ain' had tam till now!"

At the bunk-house he tumbled into bed as soon as his boots were off, and was snoring in half a minute.

Dan worked around the mill the rest of that week. Bill Bean, the pit-man, had been careless about a splinter in his hand, and was suffering with an infection. It was Dan's job to help him take the boards away from the pit and balance them across the axle of a pair of high wheels. When a thousand feet or so were on the rig he would tie a rope over the load and haul it out to the sticking-ground, where Jotham Grant stacked the lumber in neat piles.

It was not especially difficult work, and Dan had time to watch the smooth performance of the mill-crew. The main requirement of his job was to keep the pit clear, so that the marker need never have any trouble in sliding the boards off the rolls. He had

DAN HAD NEVER SEEN

A CROSS-CUT BLADE FLY SO FAST

heard many tales of 'Poleon Duval's prowess, but this was his first opportunity to see the one-armed man in action.

As each plank fell forward from the saw, the tall Frenchman would scribble a figure on it with a huge, soft crayon. He could estimate the number of feet in a board with uncanny speed and accuracy. The pencil swung on a string, fastened to his belt, so that with a single movement he could mark the plank and heave it along the rollers, into the pit. As each log was finished, he tallied its footage on a sheet of paper tacked to the wall behind him. Then, while the sawyer and roller-on were adjusting the next log to the carriage, Duval would seize a slab or two from the pile at his feet, and saw it up in two-foot lengths for the fire-box of the boiler. He never sat down or stopped working for an instant. And as Buckalew had said, he was as deft and powerful with that one arm as any ordinary man could be with two.

There was no lack of timber coming out of the woods now. Pete Brosseau, wholly recovered from his spree, was engaged in a mighty contest with Leo Duquette to see which gang could send down the biggest quota of logs. The haulers were constantly on the jump, and only the perfect team-work of the mill-crew kept them from being swamped by the avalanche of pine.

Ole Jenson toiled like a beaver between the slab-pile and the engine. It took cords of green slabs a day to hold a full head of steam on the old boiler. From morning till night the pistons galloped and the great saw whined its hungry song.

The fair weather held through most of the month. A warm spell came and melted away the snow except for a few patches sheltered by the woods. But the scoots were still able to make good time over the moist, muddy track they had worn. Buckalew was in excellent humor, for the saw-tally was running even heavier than he had expected. Week after week they averaged 120,000 feet or better.

"The way everythin's goin'," he told Judge Garland, "it 'pears too good to last. I never see a crew work like this one. Hosses all in good shape. B'iler holdin' together. Lumber pilin' up out there a mile a minute! All we kin do, I guess, is crowd our luck, an' pray it'll keep up."

The Judge had driven up, the night before Thanksgiving, to carry his grandson back to Green Hill. He laughed at Buckalew's words.

" 'Tain't so much luck," he answered, "as it is the place you're workin'. Tall, straight timber, an' good, clean sawin'. I thought right along you'd break all records when you begun cuttin' the Garland pines."

Dan came out of the pit at the sound of the evening whistle and greeted his grandfather. "Better not shake hands with me," he laughed. "The pitch works right through these cotton gloves. I'll have to scrub it off with lard when I get home."

They bundled into the light wagon, wished the camp a happy Thanksgiving, and sped away behind the eager mare. There was mellow light from the kitchen windows when they entered the Garland yard.

"Debbie's been at it all day," chuckled the Judge. "She aims to make this the high mark in Thanksgivin' dinners. Tries to outdo herself every year!"

Dan relished the luxury of his own bed that night, and slept till broad daylight next morning.

"That's all right," Debbie told him, when he rushed contritely downstairs. "The Judge figgered you could stand a rest, an' told that Frenchie to be on hand fer the chores. Ain't a thing fer you to do from now till dinner-time, 'cept git up an appetite."

About eleven Dan's Uncle Henry Davis, his Aunt Jane and their two small daughters drove into the yard. They had come twenty-five miles, all the way from Concord, for the family feast. Aunt Jane at once snatched off her things, slipped into an apron and joined the bustle of preparation in the kitchen. Uncle Henry sat down in the office to talk politics with the Judge. And Dan attempted to amuse the little girls by showing them the chickens and pigeons, the cow and other barn-yard sights.

It was a merry company that sat down to dinner at two o'clock. Debbie's turkey was a golden-brown masterpiece of juicy tenderness. There were five kinds of vegetables besides the cranberry sauce, and a heap of the feather-light "pocketbook" rolls for which the housekeeper was famous. For dessert they had mince, apple and pumpkin pies. At the end of that meal it was a task even to rise from the table.

Dan worked off some of the over-stuffed feeling by helping the women-folk wash the dishes. Then everybody gathered in the living-room to munch walnuts around an open fire.

The Judge leaned forward in his arm-chair and beamed on the assemblage.

"Danny," he chuckled, "—and you little girls— d' I ever tell you about your great-grand-uncle Frank, an' what he done, one Thanksgivin'? I know Henry, here, has heard the yarn, but I don't recollect ever tellin' it to you.

"Ye know the old Garland farm-house used to set back where our hen-yard is now. Back about 1820 it was one o' the handsomest places in the state. A big, old ramblin' house with fireplaces in all the rooms, an' one huge one in the kitchen. Most as tall as a man, it was, an' plenty wide enough to burn cordwood, whole. They lived mighty well in them days, too. Their own hams an' sides o' bacon hung from the rafters. Big bins o' potatoes an' apples down cellar. Out in the poultry yard there was chickens an' geese an' turkeys cluckin' an' gobblin'. Right beside the house I mind there stood a big sickle pear tree, more'n two foot through. It bore fer seventy years, my father told me—every fall a whole wagon-load o' pears, none of em much bigger'n walnuts, but sweet as honey.

"There was plenty o' work for the whole family on a place like that. The men an' boys tended the ani-mals an' farmed the land. All the jobs like cultivatin' an' mowin' had to be done by hand, them days. An' the women an' gals was kep' busy too. They spun their wool an' their flax, an' wove it up into cloth on big wooden hand-looms. They didn't have to depend on stores fer things, but they had plenty an' lived comfortable.

"My Gran'father Garland, I've heard said, was a powerful strict an' upright man. He b'lieved in discipline an' all the youngsters had to toe the mark.

Frank was the youngest of half a dozen big strappin' boys. He was fourteen when the evenin' of this partic'lar Thanksgivin' Day came 'round, an' I guess he'd enjoyed himself. Prob'ly had about as much to eat as any of us, an' throwed a lot o' snow-balls, an' maybe gone sleddin'. Anyhow he was tuckered out by nine o'clock, an' just startin' to turn in, when his father called him.

" 'Frank,' he says, 'before you go to bed, s'pose you rake up the fire an' fix it to keep over night.'

"The back-log should ha' been brought in 'fore dark, by rights, an' it shouldn't ha' been left fer the youngest one to carry. But Frank, he went to the door without his hat, an' started to git a log out o' the woodpile. It was dark an' cold an' all the big ones seemed to be frozen down. After stumblin' 'round awhile he got hold of a loose stick a little thicker'n his arm an' lugged it in.

"The old man was still settin' there, front o' the fire. When he saw the stick his face got sort o' stern. He stood up an' got a hoss-whip out o' the corner an' laid it around the boy's legs four or five times, pretty hard. Frank bit his lips but didn't cry, nor speak a word. When his father was through he hung up the whip again an' said, 'Now go get a back-log, not a tooth-pick.'

"Frank put on his cap an' coat an' mittens. He went out an' stayed just seven years. No Garland ever heard a word of him till he was twenty-one, an' his own man. Then, after dark, on Thanksgivin' night, he come back. He peeked in the window an' saw his father an' mother an' most of his brothers an' sisters, settin' round the fire.

"He was a big feller now, strong as a bull, with good clothes to his back, an' money in his pockets. He went to the wood-pile an' dug out the biggest, heaviest log he could find, carried it straight in an' laid it down on the hearth. 'Here's yer back-log, Father,' he says.

" 'So 'tis,' says the old man. 'I 'most have a mind to whip you, though, fer bein' gone so long after it.' 'Better not, Father,' says Frank. 'I don't b'lieve you're big enough now.' An' his father laughed. 'No,' says he. 'Anyhow, I ain't goin' to try, fer I've done it once too often already.' "

As the Judge finished his story the little girls were leaning forward, big-eyed. "Goodness, Grandpa!" said one of them. "Seven years! Where was he all that time?"

Judge Garland chuckled and went to an old secretary that stood at the foot of the stairs. When he came back he held a small object in his hand.

"Uncle Frank was never one to tell much about himself," he said. "But I have my own idee o' where he was. When he come to visit us once he gave me this—"

In the old man's hand they saw a tiny elephant carved in green jade.

"Said it was a souvenir of his runaway days," the Judge continued. "So I've a notion he must ha' been to China or Ceylon—some o' them places. Unless I miss my guess he walked all the way to Portsmouth, or maybe even Salem, an' shipped as cabin-boy aboard a tea-clipper. Frank raised a family o' boys himself, an' made 'em mind too. But so far's I know he never laid hand on one of 'em."

VII

Coming back to camp on Friday morning, Dan was glad to see all the men on hand and busy. He knew that Buckalew had been worried for fear some of the younger fellows would go off on a spree over the holiday.

"Had a good day here," the mill-man told the Judge. "Tim Gargan done it. Gave the boys a real turkey dinner with all the fixin's. Best job I ever done for myself was hirin' that cook. The only ones that went home was the married men with families—Whipple an' Rollins. The rest spent the day rasslin' an' pitchin' hoss-shoes. Duquette an' Brosseau can't hardly wait to git to choppin' again. Reckon if I'd let 'em they'd've gone in the woods yesterday!"

When Dan reached the sticking-field with his first load of lumber, Jotham Grant was nowhere to be seen. The boy dumped the boards by the simple expedient of untying the rope and giving a heave under the forward end of the load. He had turned the team and was on his way back, when he met the farmer, hurrying up from the barn.

"Dad burn it!" panted Jotham. "There was a loose board in the side o' my corn-crib that I'd been meanin' to fix, an' last night somethin' got in there. Carried off more'n a bushel o' corn. Looks like 'coon-tracks to me. The 'coons is generally all denned up 'fore this, but this spell o' mild weather has prob'ly kept 'em out later'n usual."

Dan was keenly interested in this news. He had never been on a 'coon-hunt, though he had heard plenty of stories about the sport. Later in the day, when Ben Buckalew came past the saw-pit, the boy told him about the robbery of Grant's corn-crib.

"Hmm!" said the lumberman. "S'pose you an' me take a look fer him tonight. I've got my shot-gun in the shanty, an' one o' the farmers down the road has a 'coon-dog he claims is sure death."

After the chores were done and supper eaten, Dan came up to the shack-on-wheels. Buckalew was inside, cleaning his gun by the light of an oil-lantern. Tied up by a leather thong to his chair was a lop-eared hound with mournful eyes.

"Well, Danny," grinned the boss, "I got the dog. 'Bout three minutes an' we'll be ready to go. May have to do some choppin', so you better carry an ax."

Buckalew took the gun and the lantern, slipped a handful of shells into his coat-pocket, and they started. Down by the corn-crib the big hound showed signs of interest. Nose to ground he set out along the side of the stone-wall that divided two fields. The trail led northward toward the woods, zig-zagging sometimes to follow the cover of brush and fences.

After half a mile they found themselves in the lower edge of the timber-lot, close to the brook. The dog was moving faster now and giving an occasional eager whimper. Suddenly he let out his voice in a deep, ringing bay, and dashed forward, jerking the leash out of Dan's hand.

"All right—let him go!" said Buckalew. "Can't be far now, an' we'll keep in hearin' of him."

It was not hard to do. The dog's frenzied baying could have been heard in Riverdale, Dan thought, as they ran in pursuit.

Soon the sounds changed to a series of short, yapping barks.

"He's treed him!" shouted Buckalew. And a moment later they came upon the hound leaping up and down at the foot of a big sugar-maple. The lumberman held the lantern high behind his head, peering upward into the tree.

At first they could see little, in the dim light. Then

Dan made out a furry lump stretched along a limb, forty feet from the ground. "There he is!" he cried, pointing. "Out on that big branch to the right. See him?"

"Sure 'nough!" the mill-man exclaimed. "Golly, ain't he a beauty, too? Don't seem exactly sportin' to shoot him while he's settin' up there. Ought to give this dog a chance at him. You hold the lantern an' lemme have the ax."

He took a wide stance at the base of the tree and swung the blunt side of the ax against the trunk— *wham!*

The raccoon moved nervously forward to a point two to three yards farther out on the limb. Another blow of the ax and the gray beast was teetering precariously among the smaller twigs.

"One more does it!" cried Buckalew, and drew back his arms to swing again. But before the ax descended, the animal in the tree swayed down the end of the bough and jumped.

Dan, excited as he was, and trying to hold the lantern steady, had only a confused impression of what happened next. He saw the 'coon come sailing down, his broad, furry body spread out like a parachute to break the fall. The animal landed near another tree and made for it in haste, but the dog was only a leap behind. Turning swiftly, the 'coon made ready for battle. His gray fur was fluffed out till he looked as formidable as a small bear. His wise, black-and-white-barred face was a snarling mask of fury. As the hound came charging in, he flung himself back against the tree, all bared teeth and steel claws, his powerful fore-arms raking at the dog's belly.

There was a flurry of whirling bodies and a vicious, growling, worrying noise on the part of the attacker. The 'coon fought silently but in deadly earnest. Out of the mêlée came a sudden yelp of distress, and the hound tumbled backward, his tail between his legs. In a twinkling, the 'coon was speeding toward a thicket of blackberry brambles.

Buckalew had dropped the ax and picked up the gun. Now he hurriedly raised it to fire, but the quarry had vanished before he could pull the trigger.

"Humph!" said the lumberman, and in the lantern-light Dan saw that he was grinning. "Reckon I ought to be sorry, but I can't say I am. Feller put up a plucky scrap an' deserved to git away. As fer this pore miserable critter—" he indicated the discomfited hound,—"what I'll tell his owner won't add none to his reputation."

As they started back toward the fence, the lantern

flickered low and finally went out. Dan shook it. "Guess the oil's all gone," he said. "Well, we're 'most out of the woods."

They stumbled along, feeling their way among the trees, till they reached the pasture. Even there the darkness was so thick that they made slow progress. Buckalew was leading the way and Dan, five or six paces behind, could barely make out his black shape in the gloom.

As they approached the buildings, threading a path through a clump of little scrub pines, the boy heard a sudden exclamation in front of him. There was a sound of scuffling and then the mill-man's voice. "Got ye, by thunder! Gimme that jug!"

Dan ran closer and found Buckalew tussling with a tall, lanky man. There was a crash and bits of glass flew from a rock by their feet. A strong smell of raw whisky filled the air. At that moment the intruder twisted out of Buckalew's grasp and went leaping headlong down the hill toward the brook. Snatching up his gun, the lumberman sent a load of buckshot rattling through the trees in the wake of the fleeing man.

"That'll teach the dirty skunk to come sneakin' round my camp," he growled. "Peddlin' cheap liquor to these Canucks is as bad as settin' off a powder-magazine. That's his way o' gittin' back at me, I reckon."

"Who was it—Daggett?" asked the boy.

"Yeah—the low-down whelp!" Buckalew answered bitterly. "He's goin' to make real trouble fer us unless I miss my guess."

Jotham Grant was still up when Dan returned to the house. Briefly the boy related the events of the night's hunting. "Looks as if you'd just have to nail the board on that corn-crib and hope for the best," he concluded: "And by the way, we'd better keep things locked up around the place. There's worse critters than 'coons loose." He told him about the encounter with Daggett.

"That's a fact," replied the farmer. "If I know that young devil he won't rest till he's got square, one way or another."

It turned colder the next day and gray skies presaged another storm. By night the first big flakes were falling—floating straight downward in the still air. Dan woke next morning to find a deep blanket of snow over everything. Real winter had come at last.

When the roads had been broken by the teams, Brosseau and Duquette led forth their cohorts for a big day's cutting. Dan went with them, helping to load the scoots and occasionally taking Nolan's or

Couture's place for a trip to the mill. He wore the high felt boots and buckled rubbers that were regular equipment for the lumberjacks. They were warmer and more comfortable than rubber boots and equally effective in keeping out the snow. The boy enjoyed wading knee-deep through the drifts as he guided his team along the track.

The logs were covered with snow when they came out of the woods, and Mel Rollins looked at them dubiously. "All right if it stays cold," he said, "or if we git a thaw an' it's warm fer a day or two. But any other way, they'll be hard to handle."

Dan laughed at him then, but next day he found out why the roller-on had been gloomy. The noon-day sun had softened the snow on the logs without completely melting it. And when the night freeze came on they were covered with ice.

"You'd better stay here today, an' give Mel a hand on the skids," Buckalew told the boy that morning. " 'Tain't often he needs help, but he may git behind, with them logs froze down."

There were forty or fifty sticks of pine left on the stringers from the previous day's cutting, and the first job was to roll them down to make room for the new haul, coming out of the woods. Many of the logs were so tightly frozen that even the united efforts of Mel and Dan with their peavies failed to loosen them. These had to have the ice chopped away with an ax before they could be moved. And even when they were rolled to the carriage they were treacherous things to maneuver.

One of the first necessities of good sawing, Dan discovered, was to have the log held securely on the carriage. A slip or a twist of the log and the plank was ruined, to say nothing of the havoc that might be played with the finely adjusted teeth of the saw.

For this reason Rollins kept the heavy "frost-dogs" on the carriage filed to dagger-like sharpness and sunk them into the icy log with all his strength. Dan had to learn a new technique with the cant-hook, for frequently the hinged spike would fail to take a grip until the third or fourth try.

By noon they had finished the logs from the previous day and were working on the new lot, cut that morning. There was less ice on these, so that Dan had more leisure to look around him. From his post at the rear end of the carriage he had a splendid view of the sawyer and the whirring saw. Joe Whipple was a master of his craft. He knew exactly how much pickup he had to give the engine before biting into a log. Only once that day did Dan see him stall the saw, and that was when a huge knot appeared unexpectedly in the tail of a two-foot butt-stick. Every motion the sawyer made was swift and unerring. He could tell at a glance whether the log on the carriage was big enough and straight enough to make two-inch planks, or whether he could get more out of it in inch stuff. From the best timber he sawed square-edge boards, trimming a slab off all four sides. Smaller trees and top-sticks were rough-sawn, to be sold as box-shooks.

Frequently the mill kept on running by torchlight after the chopping crews had come back to camp. Tonight, however, the sawyer stopped the engine at five o'clock. For two solid days the big saw had scarcely had a chance to cool off. Now it was necessary to go over the teeth and make sure that they were properly set.

As Dan watched, Whipple brought out his box of files and went to work. The saw teeth were of hardened steel, held in place in the perimeter of the huge circular blade by short, thick machine-screws. When he had been completely around the saw, to see that none of the teeth had been broken or worked loose, the sawyer began sharpening them. He drew the file smoothly back and forth, never allowing it to swing up or down. The quarter-inch edge of the tooth must be kept as straight and keen as a wood-carver's chisel.

"A saw's like a woman," said Whipple, with a whimsical smile. "Like a woman or a tiger, I ain't sure which. Ye have to nurse her along—humor her —wait on her. But she'll work fer ye like a fool if ye treat her square. Then when them cruel ol' teeth go snarlin' into a spruce log she's all tiger. The sound of it sends cold shivers up my back sometimes—an' I've been sawin' for more'n twenty year. Ain't no thrill like runnin' a saw, to my way o' thinkin'. If a feller likes a spice o' danger, it's there—plenty of it! Why, I've seen a green sawyer lose a hand so fast he didn't know it was gone till the saw jammed in a knot an' he needed it to reach fer the throttle."

"Gosh!" said Dan in horror. "Did you really see that? What happened then?"

"Well," replied Whipple, "he fell over in a faint,

right acrost the saw-log on the carriage. There wa'n't no doctor within twenty mile but we took him down to the b'iler an' seared the stump with a red-hot slice-bar. Sort o' rough treatment, but I reckon he'd ha' bled to death sure, if we hadn't."

The boy looked again at that great disc of polished steel—motionless now, but capable of untold ferocities—and felt a new respect for saws and the men who drove them.

VIII

DECEMBER came in, gray and blustery. A north wind blew cold for two days and then it settled down to snow in earnest. When the storm ended there was a foot and a half of solid white on the level ground and drifts as much as four feet deep along the fences.

It gave the teamsters and their horses a day of strenuous labor to break out the trails again. Even when the regular roads were open, there was trouble for the woods-crews. Drifted snow had hidden the stumps and rocks and gullies, making movement difficult. And it was frequently necessary to dig the snow away from the base of a tree before any work could be done with ax and saw.

After the tree was down, and had been cut up into logs, there was still the problem of rolling them out where they could be loaded. Dan spent most of his time, that week, plowing from one cutting to the other to help the swampers with this job. He felt himself hardening up with the work—found his flan-

nel shirts tight around the shoulders when he put
them on. His arms and back had developed thick
bunches of muscle that came from handling the cant-
hook.

Duquette's gang was now chopping on the nearer
side of the lot, getting out timber from the eastern
slope of the hill, close by the big pine. Brosseau was
at work nearly half a mile farther west. Each time
he joined one crew after leaving the other, the boy
was met by a volley of questions. "Dat punk,
Duquette—how's she mak' out?" Big Pete would ask.

"Fine!" Dan nearly always told him. "Boy, you
ought to see the logs they've got piled up over there.
They cut three trees inside of an hour while I was
with 'em."

"*Pouf!*" Brosseau would answer contemptuously.
"Dose leetle scrub stuff—w'y, a babee could cut 'im!
We got some real logs, here. Look—dat pine, she'll
cut a t'ousan' foot—mebbe some more! Hmm. W'at
you say? T'ree trees dey cut, eh?"

Then he would turn fiercely on his helpers. "Come
on, you punks! You 'ear dat? You goin' let Duquette's
bunch git ahead? Grab hol' o' dose saw, Louis. Le's
go!"

It was the same way when Dan talked to
Duquette's gang. He never had to stretch the facts.

DAN PLOWED FROM ONE CUTTING TO THE OTHER

He merely painted an enthusiastic picture of what was doing on the other side of the ridge, and Gallic imaginations did the rest.

Leo Duquette was a fiery little man with immense, sweeping mustaches which were his pride. In moments of excitement—and with him they were frequent—he would put up his hand and pull the ends of these adornments outward, first on one side, then on the other, till they bristled like a tom-cat's whiskers. His second chopper, Joe Lanoix, was a huge, hulking Frenchman, slow and strong as an ox. Duquette drove him unmercifully, and with the quick youngster, Raoul Fleury, for their swamper, they made a formidable crew.

The furious rivalry between the two groups of choppers overcame the handicap of the snow. They were felling as many trees as ever. But the mill was running below its former tally because of the difficulty of hauling the logs.

On the fourth day after the storm, Dan went to Buckalew with a suggestion.

"There's twenty or thirty thousand feet backed up in the woods now, Ben," he said. "And the teamsters are falling further behind all the time. Why couldn't I take out the spare team and help 'em get caught up? There's an old scoot down back of the stable. All it needs is a new shoe on one runner, and if you could help me fix it—"

"Come on," said the lumberman. "We'll have a try at it. That's a good idea o' yours."

Shoeing a scoot was a comparatively simple operation. Buckalew took an ax up to the woods and cut a three-inch rock maple sapling. When the branches were trimmed off, he took a straight section about ten feet long and brought it back to camp. This section he split with wedges, taking care that the two halves were even. With his ax he smoothed and leveled the split side of one of these half-rounds. Then, inserting one end under the heavy loop of strap-iron at the forward point of the sled runner, he laid his weight on the other end. The springy wood bent to fit the curve of the sled, and lay flat along the tail of the runner.

"All right," said the boss. "Hold this down till I get the spikes in." Half a dozen huge nails, driven deep through the half-sapling, held it solidly to the runner. They sawed off the extra foot or so that stuck out beyond the sled-tail and the scoot was ready.

The horses in the stable were a pair of misfits kept to replace the woods-teams in case of injury or overwork. Aside from a ration of hay and a handful of grain once in a while, they got little care from the teamsters, and drowsed in their stalls most of the time. One of them was old Jerry, a superannuated gray horse, once a famous puller, but now sway-backed and spavined. The other was a gaunt brown mare, jocularly known as Beauty. She was nervous and fidgety, covered with old harness galls, and blind in one eye. "Been mistreated shameful," Red Nolan said. "Some scurrvy spalpeen must ha' took a club to her head, onct."

An ill-assorted pair. But to Dan's eyes, as he brought the patched harness to put on them, as fine a team as a boy could wish. He got them hitched and started for the woods, riding proudly on the forward cross-beam of the scoot. It was the simplest rig im-aginable. There was no pole and no breeching. Noth-ing but the collars and traces. Long trace chains were fastened to the whiffle-trees, and the ring of the evener was hooked directly to the front of the sled.

As long as they stayed in the deeply rutted main track Dan had no trouble in managing his team. But once they reached the woods it was different. The mare was skittish, given to shying suddenly at noises on her blind side. And with the choppers hard at it, there were noises in plenty. Poor old Jerry, willing and even anxious to pull his share, was so stiff at first that he had to hobble painfully to keep up.

Dan swung the unhappy pair up the hillside toward a line of logs cut by Duquette and his men the day before. With something of a flourish he pulled to a stop beside the first log.

"Hello—Fleury!" he shouted. "How about a hand with the loading, here?"

The agile swamper came on the run, a broad grin lighting his freckled face. "Da's wan fine team!" he chuckled. "Now we git out dose timber for sure, eh?"

Heaving in unison, they rolled the first big log aboard, and the second. After that pause the horses had some trouble moving the scoot and Dan decided not to top off the load with the customary third stick. He made his binder-chain fast and clucked to the team. As there was no track broken out ahead, he found a place to turn the sled, between the trees, and started back the way he had come. The declivity ahead was steep and crooked. Dan caught a glimpse of it between the horses' heads and resolved to ease the load down as gently as possible.

A wise decision, but the fates were against him. Just as they approached the first sharp dip, there was a thunderous crash in the woods to the right. A tree coming down. At the sound, Beauty gave a startled jump forward and jerked the scoot over the crest—old Jerry lumbering into a gallop at her side.

Dan, nearly pulled off his feet, clung to the reins and started running with them. There was no way to stop the sled, now plunging downward on the heels of the frightened horses. And at the foot of the hill there was a sharp turn, where the track joined the main wood-road.

Dan had to think fast. The snow was knee-deep where he was forced to run, beside the careening sled. He couldn't keep up. And yet if he let go the lines there was certain catastrophe ahead for the scoot and possibly for the horses. With all his strength he jumped for the top of the load. He landed sprawled on all fours on the slippery logs, but with the reins still clutched in one hand.

"Hup, Jerry!" he yelled, as the poor beast stumbled, and hauling hard on the leather he managed to lift the horse into stride again. It was all he could do to stay on the runaway sled, swaying dizzily over rocks and bumps, but he still had some power to guide the terrified team. That was his only hope now —to get around that turn at the bottom. Here it came. He swung the loose ends of the reins fiercely against Jerry's rump and urged him to greater speed. Then he pulled to the right. The horses made it, swinging sharp and yanking the nose of the sled after them. But the rear end slewed wildly to the left in a spray of snow and brushed so close to a tree that Dan held his breath.

Then it was all over. The scoot lost momentum abruptly. The horses came to a panting stop. As the boy climbed off the logs to the ground he felt his knees shaking. "Whew!" he sighed. "Glad that's done with!"

Up on the ridge he saw Raoul Fleury running after them. "Hey!" cried the Frenchman, "You mak' out a' right?"

"Sure," Dan called back cheerfully. "They need these logs at the mill, and I was just tryin' to speed up delivery a bit!"

He gathered up the reins again and spoke encouragingly to the team. The mad gallop had loosened the old gray's joints and shaken some of the nonsense out of the mare. They pulled with a will and were greeted with loud applause by Mel Rollins when they brought their load to the empty skids.

"Saved the day, by ginger!" he roared. "I'll buy a feed of oats for them two crow-baits myself. Come on, Ole—give her some more slabs. We'll be sawin' again in a couple o' minutes."

It was on Thursday that Dan started driving the team. By mid-afternoon of Saturday, the scoots had caught up with the choppers, and the mill had completed two record days. As a rule, they stopped work about three on Saturdays so that Joe Whipple and the other "family men" could get home before dark. This week no one wanted to quit.

"Keep them logs comin'," said the sawyer. "We'll have a pretty good week's tally by sundown if we stick at it."

So it happened that Dan was urging his tired team into the woods for a last load, as dusk began to fall. He was hauling from the other side of the lot now, where Pete Brosseau's crew had been hard at it all week. It was wild country over there. Beyond the line-fence a forest of scrub hemlock and hardwoods stretched almost unbroken to the side of Blue Job Mountain, eight miles away.

They pulled up across the ridge and headed down the opposite slope. It was growing dark in the pines. Dan clucked impatiently to the horses and flicked old Jerry with the ends of the reins. The sound of axes ahead grew louder as they approached the cutting. There was a pause, a shout, and then the crash of a falling tree. Beauty shied at the noise as usual, and Dan spoke to her sharply and had just succeeded in steadying the team down, when there came a wild yell from the clearing right ahead.

"Gosh!" thought Dan. "Tree must have hit one o' the men!"

But at that moment they emerged into the cleared space, and he could see quite plainly what was happening. The big pine they had just brought down had struck the dead trunk of a huge old maple tree and split it squarely open. From the cavernous hollow at the roots there now thrust forth a dark, furry head, and a heavy growl reverberated across the clearing. The next instant a black bear came lumbering out, and started straight toward the little knot of excited lumberjacks, sniffing the air with lifted nose.

IX

OLD JERRY trembled and the mare snorted and reared as the scent of the bear reached them. Dan, rushing to the horses' heads, saw the Frenchmen scrambling out of the way of the brute's advance. There were shouts.

"No! No, Cantillon, you fool! *Sacre nom!* She's keel you!"

The big, young swamper had a peavy in his hand. He laughed, and with a sudden lunge, hurled it point first at the bear, which was now only a few feet away.

Like a heavy javelin, the peavy flew through the air and struck the animal high in the shoulder. There was a screaming snarl, and the bear charged blindly at the daredevil Frenchman.

Dan held his breath as Cantillon turned to jump over a log, slipped, and fell heavily in the snow. Sick with horror, the boy waited for the end. Then he saw the flash of an ax, swung by mighty shoulders. Pete Brosseau had cleared the log at a bound and struck, just as the bear reached its victim. The crazed brute reared suddenly erect on its hind feet, pawed at the air and toppled sidewise. The blade of the chopper's ax was buried three inches deep in its skull.

Dan made the horses fast to a sapling with hands that shook. As he hurried across to join the woods-crew the air was filled with their shouts. Cantillon was on his feet, unscathed, pounding the boss chopper on the back and expressing his admiration in excited French. Bergeron had crawled out from behind the stump where he had taken refuge and was dancing about them, yelling like an Indian. And Big Pete himself stood proudly with one foot on the dead bear, telling everybody within hearing how the exploit had been accomplished.

When the animal had first come out of its hollow tree, it had looked as big as a barn door to Dan. Even now, stretched in its blood in the snow, its grinning teeth were terrifying enough. But he could see that it was not actually a very large bear.

"How about getting this scoot loaded, and taking him back to camp?" the boy suggested. "It'll be dark in another ten minutes."

The Frenchmen left off chattering and began to collect their tools. Dan had some trouble getting the team any closer, but finally succeeded in steering them within rolling distance of the logs. Two sticks of pine were put aboard the sled and then, while Dan held the horses' heads, the bear was laid across the load.

There was no need to urge the ancient pair on the homeward track. Snorting and rolling their eyes in fear, they pulled the heavy scoot at a trot all the way

to the mill. When they reached the skids, the three Frenchmen tied the bear's feet together and slung the body from a pole which they bore in triumph to the bunk-house.

It was a great moment. Dan finished unloading the logs and got to the door in time to hear a babel of French patois and Yankee exclamations. Brosseau was recounting the events of the battle with appropriate growls and gestures.

Chuckling, Dan took the team to the stable and

unharnessed them. As he came out he saw his grandfather and Buckalew talking outside the wheeled shanty. Judge Garland had driven up as usual to take the boy home for the week-end.

"Did you hear about Pete's bear?" Dan asked. He gave them the high-lights of the affair while they went toward the bunk-house.

"Well, if that ain't the durndest!" laughed the Judge. "Ain't been a bear seen this side o' Blue Job in fifteen year, to my recollection. Though come to think of it, Jotham missed a pig or two, this fall, an' thought it might ha' been a bear's work."

"Looks like a young 'un," replied the mill-man, poking the carcass with his toe. "Prob'ly a yearlin'— last winter's cub."

They entered the bunk-house and once again Dan listened to an account of the bear's death. This time it was Cantillon who told it, with reverent additions from Bergeron. The tale was rapidly assuming epic proportions. It would be told in logging camps and Quebec farm-houses for years to come.

"She's fly out de busted tree lak race-hoss!" said Cantillon. "Beeg—w'y, she's look so beeg lak de church at T'ree River!"

"I'm say my prayers, me!" put in Bergeron, crossing himself.

"Straight at us, she's come—lak dees—" cried the swamper, making a horrible face and grinding his teeth. "I got peavy in my han', an' queek I t'row 'im—*bam!* On'y dat bear she's lak bewitch'. She ain' stop. Devil's in 'im, for sure. Firs' t'ing I know she's mak' jump at me—twenty foot she's sail t'rough de air. She's knock me down! On my face I feel de breath—hot! Den I see Pete comin'. She's stan' up to de bear an' look 'im in de eye. Dat bear, she's say, *'Woof!'* She's mak' swipe at Pete wit' de claws—so—but Pete, she's duck. So queek I can't see 'im, she's breeng de ax down—*pow!* De bear's head, she's spleet wide open. She's stan' up on de feet —tall lak pine tree. Den, by 'm' by, she's geev wan las' roar lak lion, an' she's fall down dead!"

In illustrating the toppling descent of the bear, Cantillon nearly lost his balance and had to be caught by two of his companions.

Buckalew heard the story out gravely and nodded at the end.

"Must ha' been a turrible scrap, all right," he commented. "I hand you boys the blue ribbon fer durnfool spunk. Don't s'pose ye stopped to figger that a b'ar, shook out of a dark hole after a month's sleepin', is stone blind fer a minute or two. If this 'un had knowed there was men around, he'd ha' skedaddled so fast ye wouldn't ha' seen more'n a glimpse of his tail."

Brosseau's face fell a little at this interpretation of the affair. But Grandpa Garland restored his beaming pride a moment later.

"I shouldn't wonder," said the old man, "if that don't actually beat the story they tell about my Great-great-uncle Lemuel. Lemmie was a big man— one o' the biggest. Weighed two hundred an' fifty— mostly muscle. At least, I guess not much of it was brains. He could lift a hoss. Used to do it fer a bet at barn-raisin's an' sech.

"Well, one frosty night in the spring o' the year, he was comin' home afoot from a dance. Road lay through the big woods, an' there wa'n't much moon to see by, but Lemmie he was feelin' good—full o' strength an' hard cider. He'd got within about a mile o' home when he saw a big feller in a fur coat settin' in the road right in front of him.

" 'Git up, ye lummox!' hollers Uncle Lemmie. 'Want to freeze to death?' The other chap grunted at him sort o' scornful and Lemmie didn't like his tone o' voice. So he ups an' heaves a rock at him— catchin' him square amidships. '*Woof!*' says the feller, an' gits on his feet, wavin' his arms like he wanted to rassle. Rasslin', o' course, was right in Lemmie's line. 'All right,' he yells. 'Durn ye, come on!'

"He grabs him 'round the body, an' my, oh my, what a chest that feller had! Turrible strong in the arms, too, an' rough—no holts barred. Fust thing Lemmie knew he felt finger-nails diggin' right through his jacket, an' the earlap of his cap was chawed most off. Lemmie'd only been feelin' playful before. Now he got mad.

" 'Hey!' he shouts. 'That ain't no way to fight! If ye want trouble, I'll give it to ye, by cracky!' An' he tries to trip him, but the feller's a sight too stout in the legs. Then Lemmie draws a deep breath an' starts squeezin' with his arms. The feller snorts an' twists, but he keeps his holt an' bends him backwards, huggin' tighter an' tighter all the time. His chin is over the other chap's shoulder, so he ain't seen his face, but he can't help wonderin' where sech a powerful man come from. After a while he feels the feller's wind begin to go out of him, puffin' an' wheezin'. Lemmie's pretty well tuckered himself but he won't own up. Jest squeezes harder, till his arms git numb.

"All of a sudden there's a sort o' snap. The feller in the fur coat goes limp an' slips down in the road with Lemmie on top of him. 'Give up?' calls Lemmie, soon as he can git his breath. No answer. 'All right,' says he, 'we'll stay here till ye do.' So they lay there on the ground a while longer.

" 'Bout sun-up a neighbor comes by with a team, on his way to mill. An' there he finds Lemmie fast asleep on top of a dead bear. Pretty fair-sized bear, too. Weighed 'round four hundred pounds, if I remember right. Folks used to tell me I took after Uncle Lemmie in the strength o' my arms," he concluded modestly. "But then most of us Garlands was powerful men."

There was a respectful pause following the Judge's story. Then Big Pete Brosseau shook his head and sighed. "Dat Lemmie," he said with admiration, "she's Canada one, eh?"

Tim Gargan had been rushing back and forth between the stove and the long table, setting out stacks of brown-bread and huge bowls of baked beans. Now he wiped his hands on his apron and stood back. "Come an' git it!" he bawled, in a voice that drowned all other sounds.

With a clatter of hob-nails and a shuffle of felts, the men trooped to their places and began the meal. There was no ceremony about it. They used their knives and forks as they handled axes and peavies— with more brute strength than daintiness. There was no conversation except such abrupt phrases as,

"Hand the butter," or "Le's see them beans, Joe."

Dan and his grandfather were about to leave, when Gargan came around the table toward them. "Speakin' o' bears," he grinned, "we had bears out in Alaska what *was* bears. That uncle o' yourn would ha' had a time huggin' one o' them big brown fellers to death. I've seen 'em bigger'n a good-sized hoss. Weighed a ton—one of 'em did. My pardner shot him right from the door of our shack. The skin was too big to go inside that twelve-by-fourteen cabin, so we had to fold the hind paws in under. We kep' our feet warm that winter. Used to wade through fur half way to our knees."

Red Nolan spoke from the table, a huge chunk of brown-bread balanced expertly on his knife. "Yeah," he said, "I've heard o' them Alaskan brown bears. Big but harmless. Wouldn't hurt a flea, they say." He winked solemnly at Whipple, who sat opposite.

"Huh!" snorted the sour-dough. "Whoever told ye that was ignorant or else a liar. Them bears is first cousin to a grizzly an' twicet as powerful. Feller on the next claim to ourn built him a log house. Built it strong an' solid, with walls a foot thick an' big rocks weighin' down the roof. One day in the spring he locks up an' starts fer Nome to pack in a grub-stake. Next mornin' we looked out an' seen a bear standin' up on his hind feet, beside the feller's shack. He must ha' been ten foot high—head an' shoulders taller'n the house. He reaches out a paw an' wipes them rocks off the top. Then he brings the paw down hard an' busts the roof wide open. After that it took him about half a minute to pull the walls apart. There wa'n't enough left of it fer kindlin' wood."

"Why didn't ye holler at him," put in Rollins. "Prob'ly scairt him so bad he'd been runnin' yet."

"Listen," said Gargan, grimly earnest. "I tell ye these big bears is mean. They ain't afeared of any man. There was an old-timer name o' Hanson in the gold camp on Mission Creek. He had a claim up on the mountain where he'd spent a winter. One day he told us he was goin' up there to git a box of old magazines he'd left in the cabin. 'Twa'n't above eight mile, an' he figgered to be back by night. We didn't see him around, next day, so a bunch of us made up a search party an' went up the trail.

"When we found the cabin it looked peaceful enough. The door was off its hinges, but the sun was shinin' in on the log floor. Right on the threshold, though, we come on his rifle, with the butt smashed, an' the barrel twisted. An' back in a corner we found a dead bear cub. Little, brown, woolly feller, not much bigger'n a cat. Had a bullet through him.

"There was a pool o' dry blood in the mess on the cabin-floor, but no sign o' Hanson. Then one o' the men looked around outside an' found a track where somethin' had been dragged, an' some more blood spots. We follered 'em mebbe a hundred yards to a thicket o' brush, an' there was what was left o' the old man. He was a turrible sight. 'Most all his clothes was tore off, an' his head was beat out flat. One arm was clean gone. We dug his grave an' buried him right there, an' while we was diggin' we come on bear tracks more'n a foot long all around the place. There was four of us, all armed an' all good shots, but we didn't stay in that neighborhood long."

As he finished, the one-eyed cook bustled back to the kitchen-end of the room and began to cut apple pies, stabbing away with his big butcher-knife so vindictively that Dan wondered if it was an imaginary bear he was slicing.

"Well, boys," said the Judge. "Danny an' me'll be late fer supper if we don't start travelin'. Good night, all!"

In the cutter, streaking for home behind the lively mare, Judge Garland started laughing to himself. "Sort o' shet the boys up, didn't he?" he said. "I thought he was gittin' off some pretty tall tales, but

I guess he's been there, right 'nough. That last one sounded like a man tellin' the truth."

December went by on wings. Working in the woods all week long, Dan hardly realized that Christmas was close at hand. There were no red-wreathed windows or decorated shops to remind him of the holiday, and it was not until he saw Cantillon laboriously addressing a package to the girl in Quebec that he began thinking about gifts. The last Saturday afternoon before Christmas he got a ride to Riverdale and purchased them. It was his own pay that he was spending. That fact gave him a special sense of delight as he chose dolls and bracelets for the little girls in Concord, a necktie for Uncle Henry and a brooch for Aunt Jane. Debbie, he knew, would be charmed with the new aprons he bought her, but he was more puzzled over a gift for his grandfather. At last he picked out a pair of handsome driving-gloves, lined with warm muskrat fur.

Christmas Day fell on a Friday and the mill shut down Thursday afternoon, not to start sawing till the following Monday. When Judge Garland came to get Dan, that Christmas Eve, there was a bushy little balsam fir to be stowed between them in the cutter. The boy had chopped it that morning and brought it in on the scoot.

"Clear night, tonight, an' a good day tomorrow," said the Judge contentedly, as they rode homeward in a red sunset. "I used to think, when I was a boy, that old folks couldn't git much fun out o' Christmas, but, by Harry, I b'lieve I enjoy it more now'n I ever did!"

And Dan, looking at the old man's beaming face, was not surprised. He understood that gift of eternal boyishness which kept the Judge's Christmas always merry.

X

THAT night they hung up their stockings to left and right of the big fireplace according to time-honored custom. The balsam they put on a box in the corner. There were no tinsel balls to use for decorations but they made it gay nevertheless. Judge Garland tied bits of colored ribbon to the stems of half a dozen shining red Baldwin apples and hung them in the branches. Dan brought out the corn-popper and soon had a milk-pan full of fluffy white kernels ready for Debbie to string on threads. Her wrinkled hands flew as fast as her tongue. By bed-time she had made yards and yards of pop-corn chains, and Dan had festooned them around the tree.

"Ho hum!" yawned his grandfather. "'Most eleven. Later'n I've been up in months. You put out the lights an' lock up, Danny, 'fore you go to bed. I'm goin' to turn in."

As he reached the foot of the stairs a jingle of sleigh-bells sounded loud in the driveway.

"What in Sam Hill—" began the Judge. "Don't

tell me it's Santa Claus come to fill those stockin's!"

Cheerful voices called from outside. "Dan! Oh, Dan Garland! Come out here!"

Dan opened the door. In the starlight stood a team and a pair of bobs with a hay-rack body, half-filled with straw. A dozen boys and girls of his own age were sitting in the straw, laughing and chattering.

"Git your things on, Dan," called one of the youths. "We're goin' carolin', down the Farmin'ton Road. Git ye back by two o'clock."

Dan turned back to the lamp-lit room.

"Sure, go 'long if you've a mind," grinned the Judge. "I'd like to go with ye, if it wa'n't fer the cold gittin' into my j'ints."

The boy hustled into his mackinaw, cap and mittens. "I'll be back in a couple of hours," he said. "Merry Christmas to you and Debbie!"

He swarmed over the rail of the rack and made a place for himself, burrowing his legs deep in the straw. And to the accompaniment of squeals from the girls and laughter from the boys, the team swung the big sled back into the highway.

Dan had a good baritone voice and liked to sing. Jogging down the road they harmonized on old favorites like "Jingle, Bells," and "Seeing Nellie Home." As midnight approached they found themselves in a fertile farming section five or six miles from Green Hill. Big barns and snug houses, dark now in sleep, clustered close to the road. The boy who was driving struck a match to look at his watch.

"Right on the dot," he murmured. "Let's start with 'God Rest Ye, Merry Gentlemen.' Give us the pitch, Garland."

Dan hummed the first bar softly. A moment later the old carol was ringing out in joyful harmony on the still night air. Windows were raised in farmhouses as they went along, and voices came across the snow, wishing them a Merry Christmas.

About one o'clock they turned the sled westward and started for home by a different road. The farms grew more scattered and the singing intermittent. With sleepy giggles the crowd was pairing off—boys holding girls' hands and snuggling close together against the cold.

Dan said good night and climbed out at a crossroads half a mile from Green Hill. His legs were stiff with sitting and he ran the first part of the distance to warm himself up. Ahead of him the Garland place and its buildings loomed dark and still. He knew that Debbie would leave the kitchen door unlocked for him, so he tip-toed past the front of the house and around to the back porch.

It was just as he had mounted the steps and laid his hand on the door-handle that he heard a sound from the direction of the barn. A muffled scrabble of hoofs and a nervous snort. Babe, usually a quiet sleeper, must have been startled by something, he thought. Perhaps a rat had run through the stall. He'd have to set a trap in the morning.

In another moment he would have entered the house. But before he could turn the knob another sound came to him, very faint but unmistakable. It was the mutter and squeak of a rolling door being pushed slowly open, an inch at a time.

It was too dark for Dan to be sure but he thought he saw a streak of deeper blackness at the edge of the stable door. He crossed the yard on stealthy feet. His eyes hadn't deceived him. The heavy door had been pushed back about a foot. A warm, horsy smell came out to him and he could hear a quick pawing of hoofs just inside. Someone had taken Babe out of her stall—she was there in the open barn-floor!

For the space of a few seconds Dan hesitated, his ear laid close to the door. From within he heard the clink of a buckle and a man's voice whispering, "Hold still, you—git over there!"

Cautiously the boy edged up to the opening and slipped through. Without making any noise he moved quickly to one side so that his body would not show in the doorway. Babe must have seen him for at that instant she gave a glad whinny. The man swore under his breath and hastily clapped a hand over her nostrils. Dimly Dan could make out his outline as he moved on tip-toe to the door. A big, slouching fellow, half a head taller than the boy himself.

Fervently Dan wished for a weapon of some kind. There was a pitchfork stuck in the mow at the rear of the barn, but that was too far to go. The man had the end of the halter rope in his hand and was pulling the mare after him. Another moment and he laid hold of the door to slide it farther open. His back and shoulder were toward Dan as he tugged at the edge with his free hand. Now was the time! The boy sprang on him, flinging an arm about his neck and jerking him backward.

They fell heavily together on the floor. Taken completely by surprise, the thief lay stunned for a second, and Dan squirmed over on top of him. His hands clutched for the fellow's throat, but before they could find a grip, the wiry body under him gave a sudden twist. A knee struck him in the back, and then they were rolling over and over in the choking dust, grappling desperately for holds. Just what happened next was never quite clear in Dan's mind. There was a crash and a blackness shot with stars. Then he sat up, his head ringing, and found himself alone. Struggling to his feet, he staggered to the door. There was a dark figure running past the house, heading for the road.

"Hey!" yelled the boy, as loudly as he could. "Stop or I'll shoot!"

The man only ducked low and ran faster. In another moment the thud of his foot-falls had died away. Back in the barn Dan found the frightened mare and calmed her. She had jerked the halter out of the thief's hand at the beginning of the struggle and retreated to the other end of the floor, snorting and trembling. As he patted and stroked her side, Dan's hand encountered a folded blanket and a strap, buckled tight around her middle. The man must have meant to ride her, once he had led her beyond earshot.

Dan removed the strap and the pad, put Babe's night-blanket back on her, and took her to her stall once more. What to do next he wasn't quite sure. There was no way to lock the barn door. And with the throbbing in his head still reminding him painfully of his recent experience he had no wish to leave the mare without protection. Finally he decided to stay where he was the rest of the night. He shut the door tightly and went to sleep in a pile of hay close by Babe's stall.

The three or four hours' slumber he got before daybreak were not very restful, but his head felt better when he woke. Before doing the chores he went to the house. He was washing his face in the kitchen when Debbie came down.

His "Merry Christmas!" was met with a scornful cluck.

"I heard ye come in," said the little housekeeper crisply. " 'Most seven o'clock—a fine hour to be gettin' home from a straw-ride! Why, when I was a girl my paw'd have took a switch to me if I'd stayed out past midnight. What these modern young folks is comin' to, I'm sure I don't know. An' look there—straws still stickin' to yer jacket!"

"Whoa!" laughed Dan. "Steady up, Debbie! I know you won't believe it, but I was home at two o'clock. Slept out in the barn. Had a scrap with a horse-thief first, but he got away. Here—feel o' this!"

Debbie's gnarled fingers explored the back of his head, where he pointed, and she gave a little cry. "My lands, Danny! That lump's bigger'n a hen's egg! A hoss-thief, did ye say? An' here I was callin' ye names fer keepin' late hours! Quick, let me put a compress on it!"

"Nothing doing," the boy grinned. "I've got chores to do, soon's I get into my barn clothes. Don't scare the Judge, now! They didn't get Babe. She's safe in her stall and no harm done."

When he returned to the barn the sun was up and the barn floor was light enough to see evidences of last night's struggle. For yards around, the dust and hay-straws had been swept clean by their threshing bodies. But he looked in vain for anything that would give a clew to the stranger's identity. It was only when he was coming back to the house with the milk that he found what he was after. As he opened the barn door, the wheel on which it rolled stuck for a moment. He reached down to free it and picked up a red knitted cap, old and dirty.

Where had he seen such a cap before? Somewhere—and under unpleasant circumstances, he was certain. Still holding it in his hand he crossed the yard and went into the kitchen.

"Did ye see the man good 'nough to recognize him?" asked Debbie in a stage whisper.

"No," said Dan, frowning and trying to think.

"I jest wondered," the housekeeper went on, "if it could ha' been that wu'thless young Daggett. Ye know he's—"

"Of course!" Dan exclaimed, his face clearing. In

a flash he saw that cap picked up by Buckalew and stuck roughly on the vagabond's head, the night of the bunk-house fight.

"This is his," the boy explained, holding out the cap. "I was trying to place it and couldn't remember. I should have thought of him first of all, I guess. The dirty thief! After Grandpa had worked so to get him that job, too!"

"What's all this?" cried the Judge from the doorway. "Merry Chirstmas! What d' you s'pose is in them stockin's?"

Dan's face was rueful. "Gosh!" he exclaimed. "You two stay here in the kitchen a minute and don't peek. I forgot something."

He dashed upstairs and found the gifts he had already wrapped and hidden in his bureau drawer. Hastily he stuck them in the tops of two awkwardly stuffed stockings by the fireplace.

"All right," he called. "I guess Santa paid us a visit last night after all!"

They took their presents to the breakfast table and opened them with exclamations and laughter. As usual, Debbie had given him something both welcome and practical—a pair of warm mittens and a muffler, knitted by her own busy hands. His gift from Judge Garland was a beautiful pair of racing skates.

"You won't have much time to use 'em this winter," the old man smiled. "But wait till you git to Dartmouth! Plenty o' skatin' there, I'm told."

After breakfast, Dan told the Judge what had happened in the night. His grandfather showed that he was shocked, but heard him through in silence. Then he shook his head. "Ain't been a barn locked in this county fer thirty years," he said sadly. "But I'll get the best padlock I can find, today, an' we'll make that door fast. No, I don't aim to have Ike Daggett arrested. If I knew where to find him, though, I sure would like to talk to him."

That afternoon Dan drove with his grandfather to Riverdale. The hardware stores were closed, of course, but the Judge went to the home of one of the dealers who was a friend of his and explained his need. They came away with a heavy steel bar and staple and a big, well-made padlock. And when the chores were done that evening, the barn was as solidly locked as a bank vault.

Dan had a chance to use his skates on the river next day. There was a big crowd of youngsters out, making merry on the smooth, thick ice. There were several impromptu brushes between the older boys, and though Dan had to get used to the long, straight blades of his racing skates, he found he was soon able to leave the rest behind with ease.

They picked up sides for a hockey game later, and when the early dark came, there was a huge bonfire built, close to the shore. For another hour or two they skated by its light. Dan was getting hungry and had about decided to start for home, when he saw a big, lanky youth buckling on a pair of old skates, in the edge of the firelight. It was Daggett. Dan skated nearer, looking at him closely. His untidy shock of black hair was uncovered, and he had one mitten off, to fasten the skate. The knuckles of his hand showed bruises and scrapes.

"Hi, Ike," said the boy. "Where's your hat?"

The fellow looked up with a sudden start. His face was scowling as he saw who had addressed him. "Pretty fresh, ain't ye?" he growled. "If ye knew beans, ye'd know I never wear no hat."

"That right?" asked Dan coolly. "I thought I remembered seeing you in an old red skating cap."

"Well, ye didn't," muttered Daggett, and then, wrathily—"Go on—chase out o' here, 'fore I bust ye one!"

"You and who else?" jeered Dan, but at that moment a boy at the end of a string of skaters grasped his hand for a game of snap-the-whip. When he looked in that direction again, the lanky good-for-nought had left the ice and was going off, up the hill. Dan thought of following him to see where he could be found. He was surer than ever now, that the horse-thief was none other than Daggett. But there had been an ugly look in the fellow's eyes. Now that he knew he was suspected, he might prove a dangerous man to tackle, single-handed. Prudently, Dan took a round-about way home, instead of going by the short cut, directly through the woods. When he came within a hundred yards of the house he was glad he had used discretion. For back at the edge of the woods the faint light of the new moon showed him a dark shadow, sneaking off across the snow.

XI

AS NEW YEAR'S approached, the routine of the lumber-camp, broken for the holidays, was in full swing once more. A spell of bitter cold weather shut down on the north country in those last days of the old year. The thermometer by Grant's back door read 35 below zero when Dan left the house Tuesday morning. The barn pump was frozen and water had to be carried from the house in buckets for the stock. The boy dressed in his warmest clothes and wore his new mittens and muffler, as well as a cap with a heavy ear-piece that came down over the back of his neck. Even so, he found his nose and cheeks numb with cold before he had been in the woods half an hour.

"Keep rubbin' 'em," counseled Red Nolan. "Pull yer muffler up over yer chin, too. An' don't stand still in one place or yer toes'll git frost-bit. I was haulin' cordwood one winter—a ten-mile pull into Riverdale. Had a bag o' straw to put me feet in, too, but one night when 'twas cold like this I got down off the load an' couldn't stand up. Feet was no bet-

142

ter'n a pair o' stumps. The fellers at the wood-yard got me felts off an' rubbed them bare toes with snow till I thought I'd bust out yellin'. It saved 'em though."

The choppers were extra careful with their tools, Dan noticed. At night they carried them all into the bunk-house and stacked them in a corner. The biting cold was likely to make a finely ground ax-blade as brittle as glass. When Pete Brosseau was ready to use the saw, he always wrapped the head of his precious ax in an old mitten before laying it down.

Those cold nights, when the boy lay huddled under a heap of comforters, he could hear the booming and snapping of the frost, far away in the forest. Through the still, icy night would come a sudden crack like the report of a rifle, as frozen moisture swelled and split the crotch of some big tree.

Ole Jenson kept a slow fire of big knots and maple chunks going all night under his boiler in such weather, so that the water wouldn't freeze. Dan worked hard all day Wednesday and was so tired that he went to bed early. By midnight his first heavy sleep must have been over, for he roused suddenly at a noise outside. Jack, the big collie, was barking furiously. Dan knew that the dog was shut inside the barn on cold nights, and his first thought was of Daggett. Could he be trying to steal some of Grant's stock?

Springing out of bed, the boy went to a low rear window under the eaves and peered out. There was no one in the barn-yard. Gradually the dog's barking subsided to a series of grumbling growls and silence fell again.

"False alarm," thought Dan, and went back to his warm covers. But in the morning he had reason to change his mind. Up at the mill he found Ole swearing mighty Swedish oaths and hurriedly raking the smoldering wood out of the fire-box. An ominous rumble was coming from the boiler itself, and the safety valve was spouting steam with great violence.

"What happened?" asked Dan.

The Swede pointed under the boiler and went on dumping the fire. A thick icicle hung from the outlet spigot, and beneath it was a great pool of solidly frozen water.

"Ay bane pretty lucky, Ay tank," said Ole. "Some faller come in night, an' tie down safety-valf wit' wire, an' let out water, too. Ay tank he wan's b'iler to blow up. Only water is freeze in spigot first. Ay find gauge yoompin' oop like crazy!"

Dan looked about swiftly. But the hard crust had been trampled by so many feet since the last snow that there was no hope of finding the mischief-maker's tracks.

Buckalew was furious when he heard what had happened. He had seen boilers blow up before, and men killed by them.

"We've got to stop this dirty rat," raged the lumberman, "or he'll send some of us to the hospital. Maybe he's been monkeyin' with the saw or the engine. I'll go over 'em with Whipple, 'fore we start work."

That afternoon the boss arranged with Jotham Grant to have the collie kept at the mill. A comfortable bed of old blankets was placed for him in a box behind the marker's platform. And though the dog seemed a little distressed about leaving the farmhouse unprotected, he understood his master's stern commands. When dark came he obediently took over the job of guarding the mill, and from that night on, the mill was undisturbed.

New Year's Day was a holiday particularly dear to the hearts of the French Canadians. On Thursday evening the choppers and swampers, Duval, the marker, and Couture, the teamster, laid out all the finery in their duffle-bags and prepared to start for Riverdale. All night they would dance with the pretty

French factory girls and on the morrow they would go to Mass in the big French church.

"Seems as if us Yankees ought to figger out some way to celebrate," said Mel Rollins, regarding the preparations with a jaundiced eye. "Me—I'd like to gamble a little on a hoss-race, if there was any decent hosses."

"Shucks," answered Whipple. "The two best hosses in this end o' the state is right here in camp, this minute. What d'ye say, Ben?"

Buckalew was talking to Judge Garland just outside the bunk-house door. "Eh?" he asked. "What's that about hosses?"

The big sawyer grinned and squirted a stream of tobacco-juice into the sawdust box by the stove. "I was jest thinkin'," said he, "that I'd like to bet a few days' pay on that black mare o' the Judge's agin your roan."

A light twinkled in the lumberman's eyes. "I dunno," he drawled. "Sort o' hate to take a workin' man's money. Besides, if the brush was tomorrer, the Judge wouldn't have time to send fer a good racin' driver."

Judge Garland gave him a shrewd look and winked at Danny.

"That's true," he nodded. " 'Twouldn't hardly be

fair to Babe to have a dodderin' ol' fool like me handlin' her. You'd prob'ly want to give odds in that case, Ben—say two to one."

Buckalew shrugged, knowing he had been fairly caught. "Good enough," he said. "I'll make it ten dollars to five, in a trot from Grant's to your gate in Green Hill. 'Bout two miles an' a half, ain't it? Only one thing—I think 'twould be safer if you carried Danny along—somebody to take holt o' the lines in case o' trouble."

The Judge started to bristle, then calmed himself. "Reckon you're right, Ben," said he. "Long's you're choosin' a side partner for me, I'll nominate Jotham Grant to ride with you, an' we'll drive this race at ten-thirty tomorrer mornin'."

There was a titter in the bunk-house. Jotham Grant weighed upwards of two hundred pounds and was nearly as broad as his own barn-door.

"Done!" snapped Buckalew. "I'll need some ballast when ol' Major starts flyin'. Jotham's the man I'd ha' picked, myself, if I'd had the choice!"

Solemnly Judge Garland shook hands with Major's owner, and he and Dan left for Green Hill. "So-o-o, gal, so-o!" he crooned to the mare as he eased her down the hills. "Ain't no p'int in gittin' all used up, tonight. Want ye in pretty good shape in the mornin'."

After a while he turned to the boy. "Dunno, Danny," he sighed. "Mebbe I've bit off a leetle more'n I can chew. Ain't as young as I think I am, an' neither's the mare. She'll give him a race, but that's a powerful hoss—that Major."

When morning came, however, the Judge's doubts appeared to have vanished. His face at breakfast was as serene as the New Year sunlight on the snow. He accompanied Dan to the barn to supervise the little trotter's grooming.

"Look at that!" he chuckled, as she tossed her pretty head and whinnied. "Couldn't act spryer if she was a two-year-old. Brush her good, boy. When the sun shines on that coat o' hers, Ben'll know he's lookin' at a race-hoss."

They went over the harness and oiled it carefully, then inspected the cutter. It was light and strong, built for use rather than for racing, but not much of a weight to pull on good snow. Under his grandfather's direction, Dan took a sheet of emery paper and rubbed the bearing surface of each runner till it gleamed like a mirror.

By nine-thirty they were ready. The Judge put on his old sealskin cap, relic of his younger days, and wore the new fur-lined gloves Dan had given him. "By thunder!" he laughed, as he flexed the pliant leather—"I ought to be able to drive with these! Warmer'n toast, an' jest as easy as if they wa'n't there!"

The roads were in perfect condition for sleighing. The snow had been packed hard and smooth by more than a week of travel, and there were no icy patches to make the footing uncertain. Babe was eager to go. Gently the old man talked to her and finally steadied her down to an easier pace. About half a mile from the Garland gate they came on a load of hay blocking the left-hand side of the road. It was standing still, the horses resting, and the driver working at something under the front bob. The Judge slowed down as he passed.

"Mornin', Eph!" he called jovially. "Broke down?"

The farmer grunted. "Looks like the king-bolt's busted," he replied, and continued to strain at the forward rocker.

They went over a little rise and the hay-rack was lost to view. Judge Garland was whistling softly to himself—a way he had when considering a new idea.

In Grant's door-yard they found an expectant crowd gathered. All the Yankee contingent from the mill, as well as half a dozen curious neighbors, had assembled to see the start of the race. The big roan horse had been harnessed, and Buckalew was warming him up in a series of short dashes up and down the road in front of the farm.

He came in soon, and the horses were blanketed while the two drivers discussed final arrangements. "I'll tell ye, Ben," said the Judge. "This road ain't really wide enough to start abreast, an' rather'n risk a collision, gittin' away, I'm content to let you take the lead. There's plenty o' places to pass, further on, if the mare's got the speed to do it."

Buckalew looked puzzled. "It's all one to me, Judge, but it seems like a mighty generous offer. This Major hoss is hard to pass, I warn ye. Hadn't we better toss fer it, or draw straws?"

The Judge shook his head. "No," he chuckled, "I'll take my chances. Only rule I ask is that where there's room to pass, the front sleigh should keep to the right. That's fair, ain't it?"

"All settled, then," the lumberman nodded. "Come on, Jotham, squeeze yer big carcass in here, an' try an' give me elbow room."

Dan and his grandfather got into their own sleigh and wrapped the buffalo-robe securely around their knees.

"We'll take a couple o' minutes to warm up again.

an' then go from a standin' start!" the old man called out. "Joe Whipple, you give us the word."

With their blankets off, the two horses were trotted a little way up the road and back. Then Buckalew pulled up in front of the house, with Babe's nose a yard behind his cutter.

"All ready?" he shouted over his shoulder.

"Ready enough," answered the Judge.

"Git set!" bawled the sawyer. "An' *go!*"

The tall roan started with a plunge under the touch of his owner's whip, and the quick-moving little mare was right after him. Dan, clutching the side of the seat with nervous fingers, could see the powerful rack and drive of Major's hind-quarters as he settled into that tremendous stride of his. Buckalew's shoulders looked tense and determined, but Grandpa was sitting back, holding the reins lightly, almost carelessly. The space between the cutters widened to a couple of lengths in the first few hundred yards. Then the mare's small, flying feet picked up a good share of the distance.

Dan listened to the wind whistling past and thought he understood why his grandfather had taken the rear position. If they could keep close enough, the big horse and bulky cargo in front would break the wind for them. All well and good. But where would Babe ever find enough speed to go by the mighty roan?

Twice, when they came to wide, level places in the track, the Judge pulled Babe to the left as if he were preparing to pass. The mare thrust out her head eagerly and sped forward only to be gently checked when she was almost abreast of the other sleigh.

"Gosh!" muttered Dan. "Maybe we could have done it that time!"

But the Judge shook his head. "Let him pace us awhile longer," he answered. "This is a long race. Mare's got to be fresh fer the finish. All I want's to be sure Ben'll give me half the road when I do try."

They thundered across the bridge at Kent's Mill, that marked the end of the first mile. Flecks of foam were coming back from the roan's mouth, but there was no slackening in his gait, even on the long grade that led out of the valley. It was a hill to take the heart out of any horse. Babe gave a little ground, but she was still strong at the top, and proceeded courageously to make up what she had lost. Before the end of the second mile she was so close that they could hear Buckalew's words as he urged his horse along— so close that Grandpa began pulling her out to the left once more.

There was a little rise just ahead. The Judge leaned forward, lifted the whip and spoke sharply to the mare. His eyes were bright with excitement. "This is the time!" thought Dan, and gripped the seat edge. Inch by inch the little trotter crept alongside the other sleigh, straining every muscle in her effort.

"Keep over!" yelled the Judge and flicked the whip on her back. They swept over the top of the rise neck and neck, and there just below them, on the right of the road, was the stranded load of hay!

Dan heard Buckalew swear, saw the big roan's head jerk back to a tug on the reins. Then Babe flashed past the hay-rack and straightened out for the last half-mile, trotting like a little black whirlwind.

"Didn't upset, did they?" queried the Judge anxiously.

Dan looked back. "No," he said. "Here they come —and, man, they're coming, too!"

"Ain't afraid of 'em now," said the old man briskly. "Git goin', gal! 'Most home now—show 'em what ye can do!"

The mare seemed to understand. Her neck was stretched in a line level with her back, and her legs flew faster, faster, till it seemed as if nothing made of flesh and bone could stand the pace.

Behind them they could hear Buckalew's hard voice and the crack of his whip above the frenzied thudding of Major's hoofs. But the Garland barn was in sight now—the maple trees—at last the house —and they were close to the finish. A good two lengths still separated the sleighs when Babe flashed past the gate. She had almost turned in, and only the Judge's powerful pull on the reins prevented a smash.

When the horses had finally been turned and walked back to the house, Buckalew wore a crestfallen look. He tossed a blanket over the steaming roan, and came over to the other sleigh. "Judge," he said, "I hand it to ye. That was drivin'. An' I reckon the best hoss won, though it would ha' been almighty close, if— Oh, well, I ain't one to make excuses. Here's yer ten dollars."

Judge Garland waved the money away with a chuckle. "No, sir," he said. "Won't touch a penny of it. Ye see, I had a sort o' premonition that load o' hay would be there. I figgered Eph Hayes wouldn't be able to fix a broken king-bolt in less'n an hour. I'm satisfied the mare trotted a pretty nice race, though. Come on in—you an' Jotham. We'll see if

Debbie can't scare up enough dinner fer a couple o' hungry racin' men."

Dan unhitched the two trotters and led them back and forth in the yard till they had cooled off. Then, in the barn, he rubbed them both down and gave them water and a light feed. When he left them they were munching contentedly in adjoining stalls, their late rivalry wholly forgotten.

XII

THE MILL was working again, the day after New Year's, though only about half the woods-crew showed up that morning.

"Can't do much 'fore Monday," said Buckalew, "but there's enough logs down so's we can put in some sawin'. Only twelve thousand feet to go fer our first million. S'pose ye could hitch up that handsome team o' yourn, Dan, an' help Nolan haul some logs, this mornin'?"

The mill-man's orders were usually worded like that, but they were promptly obeyed. By noon Dan had made three trips to the woods with old Jerry and Beauty, and the marker's tally showed ten thousand feet. He and Nolan went back for another load after lunch.

"I'll be wantin' to be on hand whin they finish," said the Irishman. "Though it ain't likely to do me no good. In some camps, now, the boss breaks out a bit o' grog fer the hands whin they pass the million mark. But Ben, square as he is, don't have no time fer liquor around the job."

They brought their logs back to the mill, unloaded both scoots at the skids, and strolled over to the saw. Joe Whipple had just finished a log. He glanced at the board back of the marker. "Only three hundred to go!" he bawled. "Make it a big un, Mel."

Rollins pried two or three smaller logs out of the way and dug out a sturdy butt-stick nearly three feet through. As soon as it was on the carriage, Whipple pulled a bit of red ribbon out of his pocket and tied it in a clumsy rosette.

"Been savin' this since Christmas," he grinned. With a flourish he drew his jack-knife and, carefully surveying the end of the log, he stabbed a crevice in the wood. Into this he stuffed a fold of the ribbon.

"Right there," he announced solemnly, "is the millionth foot!"

Dan turned incredulously to Nolan. "How can he tell?" he whispered.

Red spat into the snow. "Bet he don't miss it by much," he announced.

The saw picked up speed and bit with a high whine into the log. Methodically Whipple and Rollins turned it, took off another slab, then a third and a fourth. Beautiful two-inch planks, twenty inches wide, began falling forward on the rollers. Gradually the saw neared the bit of ribbon.

"How much?" yelled the sawyer.

"Nine hunder' an' ninety-nine thousan', nine hunder' an' seventy foot," droned 'Poleon Duval, marking the plank.

"See that?" murmured Nolan delightedly. "This is the one!"

And sure enough, this time the saw cut in just behind the rosette.

"Wan meellion an' ten foot!" called the one-armed marker. At the words he tossed his cap to the roof of the mill and caught it deftly on his head.

January was a good month in the woods. The air stayed cold, rarely reaching thawing temperature, even at noon. It snowed two or three times, but the storms were of brief duration and followed by clear, sparkling weather. Dan throve on the hard work. He had never felt better in his life, and he knew that he was worth what Buckalew paid him, which gave him a sense of confidence.

His jobs varied. Sometimes he would be assigned to four or five different ones in the course of a week. Wherever someone was falling behind, the boss would send him to pitch in. This was not often around the mill, for the mill-crew was generally able to handle whatever came its way.

In the woods, however, something was always happening to throw the machine out of gear. If a horse went lame it might slow up the hauling for days. And when both chopping-crews happened to strike bad going at the same time it was almost impossible to keep the mill running at capacity. Once Joe Lanoix cut his foot with an ax, and for a week Dan worked with Duquette and Fleury in the big second chopper's place. It was back-breaking labor, but they had the luck to be cutting in a good location—among tall pines, clean of limbs and well-spaced. At the end of the week Dan was proud to find that they had held their own with Brosseau's men, and that the mill had kept above the daily average of twenty thousand feet, which was always its goal.

During this time, while he was busy from dawn till dark, and too tired at night to do anything but sleep, the boy's thoughts turned less and less frequently to Ike Daggett. At first, after the attempted theft of Babe, he had often worried about the lanky ex-convict, and what fresh harm he might be plotting. But as week after week went by, and no one reported so much as seeing the fellow, Dan concluded he must have left the neighborhood. Certainly the knowledge that Dan had found his cap in the barn would make him wary. And if it was Daggett who had tried to blow up the mill boiler, the boy decided it was simply a parting act of spite.

With the first days of February came a snow of blizzard proportions. The temperature fell below zero and an east wind lashed the countryside for two nights and a day, piling huge drifts higher than the middle sash of the farm-house windows. While it lasted there was no cutting or sawing done. The school "barge," a long covered wagon-box on sleds, was unable to get through, and to the joy of young 'Lysses he had a two-day vacation.

There wasn't much for the boys to do. The Grant barn was connected with the house by a long shed, so that no paths had to be kept open. And outside of helping 'tend the stock twice a day and keeping the wood-boxes full, their time was their own.

Dan helped 'Lysses oil his traps and mend his snow-shoes. The youngster had a trap-line on the brook, back at the edge of what was called the "big hackmatack swamp." It was only two or three miles from home, but as wild and desolate a place as one could ask. Already, 'Lysses had nearly fifty muskrat skins stretched on the south wall of the barn, and had caught one mink. By spring he hoped to have enough fur to buy a new rifle and a suit of clothes.

The storm blew away in tattered clouds on the morning of the second day, and chill sunshine sparkled over a white world. 'Lysses was out of bed with a bound.

"Hey, Dan!" he called. "It's cleared off. Won't be no school today, an' you don't have to work. Come on with me to the swamp. I bet them ol' traps is bustin' with rats!"

But Dan knew there would be plenty for him to do in camp. He got into his clothes, helped with the chores, and ate his buckwheat cakes and sausage. As he started wading up the lane he saw 'Lysses' small, stalwart figure trudging off on snow-shoes across the drifts. The boy carried a short club and a grain-sack. Jack, the collie, tried to go with him, but floundered so deep in the drifts that he had to give up. The last thing Dan saw, when he looked back from the pasture fence, was the big dog staring disconsolately after his master.

That was a hard day's work. At the bunk-house, Buckalew passed out shovels to the whole crew and gave crisp orders. First, paths were dug to the mill and the stable. Then half a dozen men were set to removing the drifted snow from the saw-carriage and the skids, digging out a space for Ole to work in front of the boiler, and clearing the pit. Meanwhile Nolan and Couture made a four-horse hitch of their two teams, and the rest of the crew got aboard the scoot. With whoops and yells they started toward the woods.

Monk and Ginger made a fiery pair of leaders. With four feet of snow on the level, their progress was a series of plunging leaps, while Duke and Prince pulled powerfully behind them. Whenever the team came to a deeper drift the Frenchmen on the scoot would rush forward, cheering, and start to shovel. It took nearly an hour to traverse the quarter mile between the bunk-house and the entrance to the timber-lot, but behind them the track was open—six feet wide and ready for hauling.

In the woods there were fewer drifts, but stumps and standing trees made the going harder. The team was given frequent rests while the swampers plowed ahead, feeling under the snow with their shovels and marking where the road should run.

By lunch-time they had reached the first cutting and three of the men were left to dig out the felled logs while the rest went on with the horses. As usual there was a good deal of repartee between Red Nolan and his plump colleague.

"Listen, Johnny, me b'y," said the Irishman plaintively. "Them jack-rabbits o' yourn is all wore out. It's a shame to mistreat 'em so, an' thim so pore an' small. Let's put a real team in the lead fer a change. Ol' Duke an' Prince is big enough so they won't have to jump clean off the ground to git their heads above the snow."

Couture waited till they reached a particularly big drift and then agreed with a grin. The teams were switched while part of the looming white ridge was removed with shovels. Then, at Nolan's shout, they moved forward, the big horses plodding straight in, till the snow was above their shoulders. There they stopped. Nolan tried to back them out for another try, but the loosened mass behind their hocks bothered them. Prince nearly sat down in the attempt. There was a half-stifled snicker from Johnny Couture.

Dan had expected to hear some fancy Irish swearing, but Nolan was patient with his team. "Come on, now, darlin's," he pleaded gently, and then—"Hup! Git in there, Duke!"

The horses plowed ahead stoutly, the muscles in their broad rumps straining with the effort. At last, with another pause or two for breath, they came puffing out on the farther side.

"Mebbe you see, now," chuckled the French teamster, "dose jumpin' hoss' ain' so bad, eh?"

When Dan went back to the mill at sunset he found a little knot of men standing around the saw-pit. Jotham Grant was in the middle of the group, his face grave and worried.

"Ain't never been gone more'n three or four hours, before," Dan heard him saying. "That's what's got Ma scared. He's smart, an' I know he can take keer of himself unless he's had an accident."

Big Pete Brosseau pushed forward. "I got some good snow-shoes, me," he said eagerly. "If I know w'ere she is—dose swamp—I go fin' de boy."

"Is it 'Lysses?" asked Dan anxiously. "I've been there, and I think I know about where his trap-line lies. Only I haven't any snow-shoes."

"Come on!" cried Brosseau. "We git 'em fer you. Fleury—she's got 'im a pair."

With Dan at his heels, he ran toward the bunk-house. In five minutes they had the long-tailed Canadian snow-shoes strapped on their feet and were ready to start. It was still light when they passed the farm-house, but Dan stopped for a lantern and matches. Then they set out, following the tracks the boy had made that morning.

In places the snow had drifted, obliterating the

THE HORSES PLOWED AHEAD STOUTLY

THROUGH THE DEEP DRIFTS

trail, but Dan knew the country well enough to keep the direction. The big Frenchman was as much at home on snow-shoes as afoot. He went at a half-trot, his powerful shoulders hunched forward and his arms swinging. Dan, less skillful, had to puff to keep up.

They crossed half a dozen farms and found where the boy had climbed a fence. From there the trail led through a rough hill pasture dotted with brush, and then down toward a forbidding line of woods. Before they entered the thick growth, Dan stopped to light his lantern.

"We're getting fairly close to the swamp," he explained, "but I don't know just where the traps start, so we've got to watch how he went."

The ground grew lower, and they could see the winding course of the brook, buried under snow. It was very cold, and though the wind had died there was still enough of it to make a mournful sighing in the tamarack tops. Dan had never liked tamaracks— or "hackmatacks," as they are called in New England. There was something ghostly and foreboding about their half-bare branches and the swaying rags of moss that hung from them. Tonight he felt their gloomy desolation like an oppressive shroud above him.

"Come on," he whispered, shivering. "We must be 'most there."

The trail swerved to the right and on the brook bank they saw where 'Lysses had dug for a trap. There was a spot of blood in the trampled snow.

"Guess he got one, right away," Dan muttered. "This is probably the start o' the line."

Following along the bank, they found at least a dozen more places where hollows had been made and traps lifted. Leaning far over, Dan could see that the traps had been carefully baited and reset under the overhanging edge of the bank. In one of them a newly-caught muskrat was struggling. Brosseau stopped to kill it and put it in his pocket.

"I don't like the look of things," Dan said, when the Frenchman overtook him. "He must have been here seven or eight hours ago, and he hasn't come back this way. As far as I know there's no other trail out, and they say there's some bad holes in the swamp —places that never freeze."

Brosseau did not reply. He was surging ahead with long strides, his head lowered like a charging moose. Panting, Dan hurried after him. For perhaps fifty paces the faint marks of 'Lysses' snow-shoes led in a straight line. Then they bore to the right again. Ahead of him, beyond the flickering glow of the lantern, Dan heard a startled exclamation from the chopper. As he stumbled nearer, the light revealed

Brosseau bending above a dark bundle in the snow.

"Mon dieu!" groaned the Frenchman. "She's froze!"

Quickly Dan set down the lantern. "Maybe there's a chance yet," he gasped. "Look, his arms aren't stiff." He snatched off his cap and burrowed his head into 'Lysses' jacket. If the lad's heart was beating it was too faint for him to hear, but he thought there was a little warmth left in the body.

Brosseau had pulled off one of the small mittens and was rubbing the stiff, white fingers with snow.

"No time for that here," said Dan. "We've got to get him home—get a doctor."

"Shut up!" growled the big chopper. "She's die too queek. No. I feex 'im. You mak' fire."

With a miserable lump in his throat, Dan got some sticks together and whittled a heap of shavings with his knife. The Frenchman in the meantime had snatched off 'Lysses' jacket and sweater, and hung them on a branch. Then, spreading his own thick blanket-coat on the snow he laid the boy on it and began rubbing his chest and sides. Swiftly, steadily, his big hands moved, while Dan fumbled for a match and nursed the flame.

Five minutes passed and the fire was burning brightly. Brosseau still worked in grim silence, the sweat dripping from his forehead. Once he glanced at the blaze. "No more wood," he said. "Won' do for git too hot."

So Dan stood helplessly by and waited, for what seemed a weary while. At last the Frenchman sat up, panting. "Come," he said. "She's 'live. Now we work on dose laig."

A faint moan came from 'Lysses' lips. Dan rushed forward and helped take off the youngster's boots, trousers and flannel underwear. Side by side, he and Brosseau rubbed the flesh, white and cold as marble, with handfuls of snow. As the boy's circulation began spreading gradually under their hands the pain must have been almost unbearable. Again and again he shrieked so piteously that Dan hesitated, only to rub with redoubled vigor at the chopper's hoarse command.

Not for another half hour would Brosseau consider bringing the frozen boy nearer the fire. Even then he was cautious about it, warning Dan against too much heat. When at last the lad's whole body was glowing an angry red, the Frenchman stood up.

"By gar!" he puffed. "We pull 'im t'rough, eh? Now we git 'im home queek. Hol' dem clo's up by de fire."

When the garments were warm, they clumsily put

them on the groaning boy. No words came from his swollen lips—only those agonizing sounds of pain. While Brosseau was wrapping his own mackinaw as a final layer around the limp body, Dan ran to the brook-bank. By the light of the lantern he made a quick search of the spot where 'Lysses had been found. Something, he was sure, must have happened to him there—a fall or a blow that stunned him, perhaps. Under the loose snow where he had been lying, Dan's hand came on a hard object. It was a sprung trap, still fastened to its clog. Two or three brown hairs were sticking in the frozen blood on its jaws. But nowhere about could he find the bag in which the lad had always carried his catch.

Hurrying back to the fire, he helped lift 'Lysses across Brosseau's broad shoulders, then tossed snow over the hot coals and led the way out of the swamp.

"We gotta go fas'," muttered the Frenchman. "Dese boy—she's pretty bad yet."

XIII

THE MOON, nearly full, had risen when at last they
drew clear of the tamaracks. It threw a bright-
ness across the snow that made Dan's lantern seem
feeble and unnecessary.

"Hey!" called Brosseau. "You go ahead queeck,
Danny. Breeng a doctor. I mak' out fine now, me."

Dan looked back doubtfully, but the big chopper
was plowing forward under his burden, apparently
unwearied. The Frenchman was right. It was still
two miles to Grant's, and, if he ran all the way he
might save many precious minutes in getting medical
aid.

As he turned and broke into an awkward trot, he
wished fervently that he had done more practicing on
snow-shoes. The thongs were already cutting into his
insteps, and his lower legs ached from the unaccus-
tomed strain. But he knew his wind was good.

Up across the bushy pasture he ran, picking his
way among the clumps of juniper and birch. The
lantern, banging and smoking at his side, was a nui-

sance. He dropped it and went on, moving faster now that his arms were free. The moonlight showed him where the smoothest going was to be found. After a quarter of a mile the hill-slope grew steeper, and he climbed the last hundred yards at a walk. The brief

rest helped him. At the top he settled to a run once more. Already Brosseau was only a moving dot on the snow behind him.

It wasn't easy to keep on and on at that awkward gait, but he couldn't forget the boy back there. His second wind came before he reached the open fields. From that point on his running was mechanical. Most of the feeling was mercifully gone from his legs. Even when he fell, as he did more than once, it was to clamber up again and resume that jerking, stumbling trot.

As he passed a farm-house half a mile from home his numb brain cleared a little. The Knowlton place, it was. They had a telephone. He swung abruptly toward the buildings, running across fences that were buried to the top strand of wire in snow. Close to the barn one of them caught the toe of his snow-shoe and threw him. A man with a lantern was coming out of the barn.

"Who's that?" called the farmer in a startled voice, and Dan, trying to answer could only make a gasping sound. Somehow he found himself struggling to his feet again and running forward. Before him a deep chasm opened and he pitched into it, unable to stop himself. It was a path that had been dug from the house to the barn. The man pulled him roughly to his feet.

"Where you goin' in such a rush?" he asked. Then —"Why, durned if it ain't young Garland! What's the trouble, boy?"

Dan's answer came in a series of broken wheezes but the farmer understood enough to hurry with him to the house. They knew what freezing was in that country.

Knowlton pulled him into the kitchen, covered

with snow as he was, and went to the box-telephone on the wall. Grimly the farmer spun the crank, listened and finally spoke.

"Gimme Doc Edwards," he barked. "Yes, in a hurry!"

His next words brought Dan a mighty relief. "That you, Doc? Knowlton talkin'. Jotham Grant's boy's froze bad. Like to die. Yeah, they're bringin' him home now. You know the place? 'Bout four mile, I should say. They got the road open today. G'by."

He rang off and turned back to Dan. "Lucky to find him home," he said. "Be there in half an hour, I guess. Road ain't too good, but that gray hoss o' his'll git through if he has to fly."

"Thanks," murmured the boy, and staggered toward the door.

"Say—hold on," said Knowlton. "You're 'bout tuckered, ain't you? Here!"

He poured a glass of milk from a pail on the table. It was still warm from the evening milking. Dan drank it slowly and felt better. "I'm much obliged," he said. "I'll be all right now. Want to get there so they'll be ready."

Ten minutes later he limped up to Grant's back door, knocked, and sat down to take off his snow-shoes. There was a quick step inside, and Mrs. Grant snatched the door open. That was what Dan had dreaded.

" 'Lysses!" she cried, peering at him in the dark. "Oh!" Her voice broke on the word.

"No, ma'am," he said quickly. "It's Dan. We found him, and he was badly frozen. Pete's carrying him home. I stopped at Knowlton's and telephoned. The doctor's on the way."

It was another quarter of an hour before Brosseau came plodding up to the door. Without a word, Jotham Grant helped him carry the moaning boy into the house and lay him on a bed. Hardly had they entered when there was a quick ring of bells, and a steaming gray horse pulled a careening sleigh into the yard.

Dr. Edwards was a brisk little man with a grizzled beard. He tossed the reins to Dan and walked rapidly to the house, carrying his medicine case. The boy tied and blanketed the horse, then went to join Brosseau in the kitchen. They could hear movements and low voices in the bedroom. After what seemed a long time, the doctor came out.

"You two find him?" he asked, and they nodded.

"Rub him all over with snow?"

"Yes," said Dan.

"That's right. Prob'ly saved his life. As 'tis he

ought to be 'round in a couple o' days. What hit him on the head?"

"I don't know," Dan answered. "We couldn't find any signs of what happened to him."

"He had a concussion," said the doctor. "Made him unconscious. Reckon we won't know till he can talk."

Dan, tired as he was, had a hard time going to sleep that night. He missed his young bed-fellow for one thing. And for another he could not help puzzling over the cause of 'Lysses' accident. A dead limb, falling suddenly from a tree? But no—there had been no tree close by. He gave up at last and slept restlessly till morning.

At breakfast Jotham Grant tried, in his slow and inexpressive way, to show Dan that he was grateful. Like many New Englanders, he grew tongue-tied in the presence of the finer emotions.

"Must ha' had a job," he stammered, "—bringin' him back."

"Pete Brosseau carried him all the way," said Dan. "He's strong as a bull, that chopper."

They continued to eat in silence till a sound from the sick-room made them both lay down their forks. It was the boy's voice, weak and faint. "Where's Danny?" he was asking.

Jotham Grant nodded and they went in together.

Mrs. Grant looked up from the bedside with an anxious smile. "First thing he said," she whispered, "he wanted to see you, Dan."

'Lysses' face, puffed and raw, stared up from the pillow. He tried manfully to grin between cracked lips. "Hi," he breathed.

Dan had trouble controlling his own voice. "Hello, old-timer," he said. "You're looking better."

"Dan," the boy whispered, "I got a mink. A big one. He was in that last trap. Did you bring him home?"

Dan shook his head. "I couldn't find your bag at all," he said. "But I'll go back and look again."

The youngster's eyes clouded with disappointment. "No," he answered. "Ike's got it, I guess."

"Who?" asked Dan, startled.

"Ike Daggett. I'd killed the mink an' put it in the sack, an' there he was, back o' me. Asked if that wa'n't a mink I'd caught, but I was scared to say yes. Told him 'twas a rat. Then he offered to show me how to skin it. I told him no, an' he come fer me. Grabbed up my club out o' the snow an' come fer me. That's the last I remember."

"Well, by thunder!" growled his father. "You hear that, Dan? Broke the boy's head an' left him to freeze to death! We got to git word to the sheriff."

Before Dan could reply, they were both hustled firmly from the room by Mrs. Grant. "The idea!" she whispered. "Rantin' like that when someone's as sick as he is!" And she shut the door behind them.

"Listen," the farmer went on. "My chores ain't finished, but soon's I'm done I want to start fer the swamp. Could you go over to Jed Knowlton's an' tell him about this? We'd ought to git four-five men together an' catch this devil 'fore he can sneak off. Have Jed phone the sheriff, too, while you're there."

Dan was glad to go on such an errand. He found the neighbors as deeply incensed as Grant himself at the news. In an hour a posse of armed farmers was ready to start, and the county officers had been notified. Dan watched the determined group set out, then went up to the camp. All day as he worked he kept an eye on the farm-yard below. And so did many of the lumber crew. At the word Dan had brought them that morning, every man had been eager to drop his tools and join the chase. Only Buckalew's calmer counsel had prevented them.

"If anybody can find Daggett," he had said, "that bunch'll bring him in. They're mad clean through, an' they can shoot straight." And no sooner had the boss finished this convincing argument than he had taken his own rifle and snow-shoes and gone after the posse.

Some time in the middle of the afternoon, Dan saw a pung drawn by a pair of lively bays turn in at the Grant gate. There were three men in the big sleigh. After a few minutes spent at the house, one of them came to the head of the lane and called Dan's name. They were the sheriff's men and wanted to question him.

Deputy Loomis was the leader of the trio. He was a big, slouching man with a lean face like a horse. Long black mustaches drooped from his tobacco-stained mouth and he wore a wide-brimmed black hat which he did not remove in the house. Strapped ostentatiously around his middle, under the open fur coat, Dan saw a big revolver in a holster.

"Now, Buddy," he drawled condescendingly, we're officers o' the law an' we ain't interested in triflin'. Make yore answers plain an' don't lie to us."

From this inauspicious start the questioning proceeded. Dan kept his temper and made his statements short and to the point.

"Now," said Loomis, "did ye ever see this Daggett, to know him?"

"Yes," Dan answered. "He worked here at the mill a while." Briefly he told of Buckalew's firing the ex-convict, then mentioned the attempt to steal his grandfather's mare.

"Hmm," said the deputy. "Why wa'n't this never reported?"

Dan explained the Judge's kindness to the youth, and his wish that he be given a chance to reform.

Loomis shook his head and looked stern. "Thought the old man had better sense," he remarked. "Comes pretty close to harborin' a criminal."

Dan was on the verge of a hot retort, but kept his mouth shut, and a moment later was allowed to depart. As he left the house the posse returned empty-handed. They had found the remains of the fire and had picked up what looked like a snow-shoe track on the other side. But the snow had drifted again in the night, and a search of several hours had failed to show the direction taken by the boy's attacker.

"It's up to you fellers, now," Jotham Grant told the deputies. "If you send out fliers all over, I reckon you'll catch him. But, by thunder, if he ever shows his dirty head 'round here again, he'll git a load o' buckshot in the stummick!"

The horse-faced Loomis patted his revolver significantly. "You jest leave that part to us," he said, and gave his companions a knowing wink. "If he's in this neck o' the woods at all, we'll have him clapped in jail 'fore he knows what hit him. So now, Mr. Grant, we'll be on our way, unless—" he winked again and expectorated in the wood-box, "—unless ye could maybe find a mite o' cider to wet our whistles."

Jotham Grant took a big pitcher to the barrel in the cellar and the whole crowd—farmers and sheriff's men—had a nip of the amber apple-juice before departing.

Buckalew shook his head as the pung jingled out of the yard.

"Can't say I set much store by anything they'll do," he said. "I've known that Hen Loomis fer twenty year, an' if they're all equal to him Daggett don't need to be scairt."

It seemed, however, that the lumberman's poor opinion of their prowess was not wholly justified. Within a week Jotham Grant had word that the ex-convict had been traced as far as White River Junction, where a yard-man had seen him swing aboard a northbound freight. Vermont officers along the Canadian line were on the watch for him and it seemed likely that he would be arrested within the next day or two. That was the last they heard, and the local sheriff finally admitted that Daggett must have escaped across the border.

"Well," Buckalew remarked with a shrug, "at least the varmint won't be 'round to bother us no more."

XIV

I T WAS more than a week before 'Lysses had recovered sufficiently to go to school. Dr. Edwards
came to see him every day and his brisk cheerfulness
kept up the boy's courage. When at last the suffering was over he gave 'Lysses a pat on the back.
"You've been a good patient," he said. "Thought fer
a while you'd have to lose a foot, or at least a couple
o' toes, but those fellows did such a fine job it wasn't
necessary. You'd better thank 'em proper, fer there
aren't many boys get as close as that to the pearly
gates an' come back whole."

The youngster remembered that advice. It was all
Dan could do to prevent 'Lysses from making him a
present of his most cherished possession—his one
mink skin. " 'Tain't as big or as nice fur as the one
Daggett took," the boy apologized, "but it's wuth
real money—mebbe six or seven dollars. I was thinkin'
o' givin' Pete Brosseau my new jack-knife—the one
with five blades an' a corkscrew, I got fer Christmas."

Finally Dan and Pete persuaded the boy to keep his treasures.

"W'y, dat was fun, eh, Danny?" said the Frenchman. "I lak fer go snow-shoein', me, an' I ain' got such good excuse fer long tam. W'at's luggin' home a leetle feller lak you! *Pouf!*"

The sledding in the woods had improved steadily with use, and the deep snow had settled enough to let the chopping proceed uninterrupted. Once more, as mid-February approached, the mill was running at capacity.

"We've got upwards of a million an' a half feet o' pretty valuable lumber stacked up now," Judge Garland told Dan one Saturday night. "Seems to me the next thing is to git some cash out of it. Guess I'll go down to Boston Monday an' see if I've forgot how to dicker."

Dan was a little disturbed at the idea. It was only a hundred miles by rail from Riverdale, but it seemed a hard trip for a man of eighty to undertake alone.

"Hadn't someone better go along to help?" he asked.

"Pshaw!" snorted the Judge. " 'Pears as if I can't have any fun at all nowadays. Why, I used to go to the city, reg'lar, years ago. Got some good friends there, too. One of 'em—Jeff Newcomb—is in the wholesale lumber business. I reckon Jeff won't mind doin' business with me, spite o' the fact I bamboozled him in a hoss-trade once."

Smiling, the old gentleman helped himself to a second piece of apple pie. Debbie, half-way to the kitchen with her hands full of dishes, looked around grimly. "Go on," she said. "Ask him about it, Danny. Ye know he's jest beggin' fer a chance to tell his evil deeds. Hoss-tradin'—humph!"

As she flounced out, the Judge gave his grandson a solemn wink. "Debbie's 'fraid you'll be corrupted," he chuckled, "but I ain't worried. This wa'n't really a very evil deed. It happened back in 'eighty-five or 'eighty-six, when hoss-tradin' was a reg'lar test of a man's intelligence. Jeff Newcomb was one o' the young sports around Riverdale, them days. Drove fast hosses an' was always lookin' fer a trade. He heard I wanted a good steady roader, so one day he stopped me in the square.

" 'Got just the animal you're after, Judge,' says he. 'Six-year old, handsome as they come.' I looked the hoss over pretty careful. He was just six, all right, an' seemed to be as sound as a nut. I drove him twice around the square an' liked his action, so I bought him fer $200 cash. Half-way home I found he was a breather. Trot him three mile an' he'd start whistlin' an' blowin' like a busted locomotive.

"Couple o' weeks later a gang o' gypsies come through. I walked my hoss down to their camp an' had a look at their string. There was only one I liked real well, an' o' course I knew there was somethin' wrong with every hoss they had fer sale. Jest the same, this partic'lar mare was a beauty. Built fer speed—pretty bay color—goin' on five. They had her hitched up to a road-cart, an' after I'd looked at all the rest I asked 'em, casual-like, if she could travel. One of 'em hopped to the seat an' took her 'round the lot at as sweet a two-forty clip as ever I see. When he come up alongside again he asked how I'd trade. 'Course, I didn't let on to be much interested. Thought I'd find out what was the trouble with her, if I could. So I strolled up to her head, pretendin' I wanted to look at her teeth again. Put my hand on the bridle an' backed her up a step or two. Minute I did that, durned if she didn't set square down 'tween the shafts. Jest a natural born setter.

"Them gypsies was sore as pups. Couldn't imagine I'd still be willin' to trade, but I acted dumb an' said I was sorry, an' s'posed it was jest an accident. Finally I give 'em my whistler fer the mare an' got $75 to boot.

"Next day I hitched her up to the cut-under buggy —bein' mighty careful not to back her—an' drove down to Riverdale. Some o' the boys were out on the river road, brushin' their trotters. I jogged along on the grass, watchin' out o' the corner o' my eye. Pretty soon I spotted what I'd been lookin' fer. Jeff Newcomb was comin' up the line. He had a hoss I knew —a big brown youngster, with a fair turn o' speed— a good stayer. I touched up the mare an' she come dancin' out alongside jest as he passed. 'Hi, Jeff,' I grinned, an' waved my whip, friendly as could be. The road was clear, ahead. He let out the brown, an' we was at it. I passed him inside of a quarter mile, and then we turned 'round an' come down again, goin' fer all we was wuth. That mare was a caution. She give his good brown hoss the prettiest lickin' y' ever see, an' when we reached the square he was four or five lengths behind. I 'most forgot her bad habits, drivin' her, an' I could see Jeff had fell plumb in love with her.

" 'Where'd ye git her?' says he, soon as he pulls up with me. I jest laughed an' told him I had to be gittin' along. 'Hold on,' he says. 'I could use a stepper like that.' 'Ain't fer sale,' I told him. But he wanted to trade so bad I finally weakened. Took his brown hoss—as honest a roader as I ever owned—an' two sets o' harness, an' $50 in trade."

The Judge's old eyes dimmed and his rotund waistcoat shook with silent mirth at the memory. "Last thing I seen as I drove off," he chuckled, "was Jeff tryin' to back the mare into the shafts of his buggy. She was settin', an' Jeff was swearin'.

"So you see, Danny," he concluded, "I know him an' he knows me. Next time we met we shook hands, to show we was all square. An' we've trusted each other ever since."

The Judge set off for Boston early Monday morning, and Dan went back to the job. It was a bright, soft kind of day, with a promise of spring in the air. Already, when the boy reached the mill, there was a sound of dripping from the eaves, and a gurgle of rivulets under the snow.

"Goin' to be a thaw," said Buckalew, looking discontentedly aloft. "Don't mind it so much, except the boys git restless, this sort o' weather. Washin'ton's Birthday comin' a week from today makes it mean, too. They'll want to go off on a bat, an' there won't be enough of 'em back on Tuesday to put in yer eye."

Dan thought for a minute. "I don't know, Boss," he said, "but maybe I can do something about that. I've got an idea. See if I can work it out."

Red Nolan was just coming out of the stable, leading his big bay team, and Dan strolled in his direction.

"Hi, kid," the red-head greeted him. "Goin' in the woods with me, this fine mornin'?"

"Hi, Red," grinned the boy. "Sure I am." The horses were brought up in front of the scoot and he helped fasten the trace chains. As he straightened up he gave the nigh horse's flank a critical pat.

"Looking sort o' thin and peaked, aren't they, Red?" he asked casually.

"What—my team?" growled the Irishman. "Ye're cock-eyed, me lad, if ye think that! Strong as elephints, they are, an' fat as butter-balls!"

"Well," said Dan, "I suppose they do look pretty good, considering the way they've been working. Funny they don't stand up under it like Couture's team, though."

"Be jabers, it's insultin' y'are!" yelped Nolan, his brogue getting thicker as his ire increased. "Thim skinny goats? Why, it's a wonder to me they don't fall down flat from the weight o' the harness!"

Dan said no more, but his smile was unconvinced. He gave the Irishman a hand with the first load, then stayed in the woods, working with Duquette's crew. At noon, Johnny Couture came by with his wiry blacks, and the boy fell into step beside him on his way back to the mill.

"Ginger looks a little off her feed," he remarked. "Getting old, is she, Johnny?"

"Huh!" the teamster exploded. "Dat hoss? She's de bes' six-years-old dis side o' Quebec! W'at you mean, boy—off de feed?"

"Oh, she's all right, fer her size," Dan apologized. "But of course she can't take this hard woods-work like those big fellows of Nolan's."

"You seein' any loads on dat scoot beeger as mine?" queried the sturdy Frenchman. "Monk an' Ginger— dey pull de shoes off dose fat hoss' any day!"

"That's hard to believe," said Dan mildly. "I sure would like to see 'em try it, though."

In the afternoon, working with the chopping gangs, he started a discussion about horses, and was highly pleased with the result. Big Pete Brosseau scoffed at the abilities of the black team. Nolan's Duke, he insisted, was a Canada chunk, and therefore unbeatable. But this opinion was far from unanimous. Fiery Leo Duquette pulled his mustaches and made an oration.

"Beeg hoss—she's lak beeg man," he said. "No good. Too slow. Dose Monk an' Ginger—dey's fight-in' hoss', by gar!"

Only by the use of real diplomacy was Dan able to calm the two Frenchmen down. "I'll tell you," he announced, as if a new idea had suddenly occurred to him, "how about a pulling-match? That'll settle the argument, won't it? We'll get Ben Buckalew to be judge, so everything'll be fair and square. And we'll have it next Monday—that's a holiday."

He went over his plan with Buckalew that night, and got the lumberman's hearty approval. Nolan and Couture were eager for the contest when they heard about it. By the next morning every man in camp was taking one side or the other, and the pulling-match was the main topic of conversation for the rest of the week.

When Monday morning came, the excitement had reached fever heat. For days the two teamsters had been currying and fussing over their horses, tightening shoes and strengthening harness. There were wagers in plenty on the result of the match. The backers of Nolan's bays were offering odds of five to three on the big team and their money was promptly covered. Not a man was missing, when Buckalew led the way to the scene of the contest.

Down by the stone wall at the foot of the pasture a lane of bare ground about thirty yards long had been cleared with shovels. At one end of it lay Jotham Grant's stone-boat, borrowed for the occasion. It looked like a big toboggan, built of solid oak planks, its flat bottom resting on the ground.

Under Buckalew's direction the men began piling the stone-boat with boulders taken from the wall. "There," he announced, at length, "that ought to be enough fer a starter. Must be 'most two ton on there now. Come on, boys, bring up yer hosses."

The teamsters had drawn lots, and Nolan was to make the first pull. He hitched a chain from the evener to a ring-bolt in the forward end of the drag, and clucked to his team. Duke and Prince bowed sturdily forward into their collars. There was a creaking sound as the harness took up the strain. Then the stone-boat began to move. When they had hauled it perhaps five paces, Buckalew called a halt. "Good enough," he ordered. "Put the blacks on."

Nervously, Monk and Ginger stepped in front of the drag and the chain was made fast.

"Hi—*yup!*" cried Johnny Couture. There was no slow leaning to the pull with this team. They snapped the tugs taut with a concerted bound, and away went the drag, to the accompaniment of cheers from the Couture faction.

"Leave 'em hitched," called Buckalew, "an' put on a couple more rocks."

The increased weight of the load seemed to mean nothing to the wiry blacks. They pulled it, and so, a moment later, did Nolan's team.

Three times new stones were added to the pile on the drag, and three times the big pair and the little pair succeeded in moving it. Finally Buckalew pointed to a huge, 300-pound stone. "Come on," he said, "we've got to settle this thing. Roll that feller on."

Room was made on the stone-boat for the big boulder, and Couture looked at it with a long face. "I dunno," he shook his head. "I t'eenk, me, dere hain' no hoss' can pull dose rock."

"What's that, Frenchie?" chortled Nolan. "You givin' up? If ye don't like it, take yer crow-baits out o' there, an' let my team show ye how!"

Johnny walked slowly to the horses' heads. He patted Monk's neck and scratched the white star on Ginger's forehead. Then he went back to the left side of the team and picked up the reins. He talked to the horses in a low, tense voice. Their ears pricked up nervously and the muscles in their shining black haunches twitched with eagerness, but they stood still. Then, as the Frenchman took a step forward, they seemed to crouch, gathering their feet under them.

"Hi-i-i-*yup!*" His voice rose to a screech on the

final syllable, and at the sound Monk and Ginger leaped ahead with a tiger-like spring. The drag followed them. An inch or two at first, then steadily moving, as the blacks surged forward with frantically pawing hoofs.

"Hold it!" shouted Buckalew. "Far enough. Now then, Nolan—your turn."

The bays plodded up and were hitched to the drag. Red's face wore a determined scowl and he was carrying a whip.

"You, Duke—you, Prince!" he shouted. "Pull togither now, ye spalpeens! Hup, there—hup!"

The big team swayed forward, straining with might and main. Their rump-muscles quivered and their shoe-caulks slipped and scraped in the half-frozen dirt. But the stone-boat did not budge. Nolan's yells of encouragement ceased, and he pulled them back to breathe.

"Give ye one more chance, an' that's all," announced Buckalew tersely.

Again the Irishman gathered his reins and spoke to the panting bays. His voice had a catch in it that was almost a sob, and he pleaded with his horses like a mother with her children. They took a fresh foothold and bowed their heavy shoulders. And just as they were beginning to pull, Nolan used his whip. The lash cut fiercely across their backs. With a mighty plunge the team went forward. The drag started—hesitated —started once more. It was the other faction's turn to yell, and they made the echoes ring.

Buckalew beckoned the two drivers toward him. "Johnny," he said to the Frenchman, "do you think them blacks o' yours can pull any more'n they have?"

Johnny kicked at a clod with his toe. "Me, I don' like fer mak' 'em try no beeger load as dat," he muttered.

"How 'bout you, Red? Duke an' Prince got all they wanted that time, didn't they?" asked the boss.

"Faith, an' 'twould be fair murder to ask 'em fer more," the Irishman replied.

"That's what I think, myself," nodded Buckalew. "I'm goin' to call it a draw. All bets are off."

And the lumberjacks, as one man, roared their agreement.

XV

EACH day, now, the sun climbed higher and shone with greater warmth. The snow, frozen every night, melted during the middle hours of the day and gradually disappeared from the open ground. In the woods, where the dark pine-shadows kept out the sun, the drifts still lay two and three feet deep, but there was mud in the track where the scoots crossed the pasture.

Dan visited the grove of sugar-maples on the south slope of the ridge. He had had an eye on them all winter, waiting for the spring sap to start running. Now he dug a hole in the trunk of one with his knife and gave a whistle of glee when he saw the clear, sweet liquid pour out in a steady drip.

For a week, 'Lysses and he had spent their evenings making spiles out of white ash sticks. They were about eight inches long and had a deep groove cut down the center. At one end they were tapered a little, so that they would stay firm when driven into the tree. An inch or more from the other end a notch was cut cross-wise to hold the bail of the sap-bucket.

The morning after he found the sap running, Dan and the boy got up at five o'clock. Carrying a lantern, a bundle of spiles and all the buckets they could hang on their arms, they went to the maple grove and set to work. In each of a score of good trees they bored a hole with an auger-bit, a yard or so above the ground. Into these holes, which were slanted slightly upward, they drove the spiles, and hung a bucket on each one.

Jotham Grant saw them coming back at breakfast-time, took one look at the auger in 'Lysses' hand, and grinned broadly. "Seems like old times," said he. "We ain't bothered with maple sugar fer a dozen years, but I guess I'll have to polish up the big kettle now."

That night the boys set a couple of clean wash-tubs on the farm sled and drove up to the "sugar orchard," as Jotham called it. Many of the buckets were half full of sap. They went from tree to tree, emptying the pails into their tubs and replacing them. Back at the house, the farmer had built a brisk fire in the old brick oven that stood at one end of the yard. Across it, two wide iron bars were laid, and a huge iron kettle, three feet in diameter, covered the top except for a smoke-hole at the rear.

THEY DROVE SPILES INTO THE TREES

AND HUNG A BUCKET ON EACH ONE

They filled it with sap and left a slow fire smoldering under it all night. The next day was Saturday. Dan asked Buckalew for the morning off, and he and 'Lysses, with occasional advice from Jotham Grant, tended the sap kettle.

"Can't make good syrup if ye let her bile too fast," the farmer told them, "An' ye have to keep skimmin' off that scum that comes on the top. Here's a ladle I made fer ye."

He gave them a long-handled wooden affair with a crudely hollowed bowl at the end. They took turns standing by the kettle and lifting ladlefuls of the thickening liquid, then pouring them slowly back.

"What do ye want—sugar or syrup?" asked Jotham after a while. "This here's thick enough fer syrup already."

"Let's make sugar out o' this first lot," 'Lysses answered eagerly. "We'll have plenty more fer syrup."

"All right," said his father. "Nip into the house an' tell yer ma to git the milk pans ready. Bring out a saucer with ye."

He made a little heap of snow beside the oven, and set the saucer in it. Then, as the boiling syrup continued to thicken, he poured an occasional ladleful into the dish. Several times when he did this, the cooling stuff merely thickened in a gummy mass. Finally, however, he cooled a batch that formed tiny crystalline grains in the saucer.

"Run, 'Lysses!" he called. "Git them milk-pans out here quicker'n scat, or we'll burn our sugar."

As he spoke he was raking the hot embers out of the fireplace. With Dan to help him he stuck a pole through the iron bail of the kettle and lifted it off. Then, as fast as they were able, they poured the thick syrup into the four wide pans that 'Lysses brought. In half an hour they were filled with huge cakes of gray-brown maple sugar.

That afternoon they collected the sap once more and started another kettle boiling. Grandpa Garland drove up before dusk, and joined in the sugaring-off with as much enthusiasm as the boys. At Mrs. Grant's urging he consented to stay to supper. That evening they made a merry circle around the roaring fire, stirring the pot and telling stories. Half a dozen of the men from the camp came to join the fun.

The Judge was in excellent humor. He had made an advantageous deal for his lumber in Boston, and had renewed a number of old acquaintanceships during his week's stay. As the patriarch of the assemblage he took over the supervision of the sap-kettle.

"Pretty fair sugar," he commented, nibbling at

a sample of the boys' handiwork. "Not quite right, though. Ain't been stirred enough to my way o' thinkin'. Now this—" and he smacked his lips over a taste of the cooking sap—"this is goin' to be prime stuff. Sweet as honey already. 'Nother hour an' she'll be ready to take off."

He plied the ladle vigorously and smiled at the ring of faces in the firelight. "My pa used to tell a story," he said, "about maple syrup. Seems ther' was a farmer over Hopkinton way, back in the old days, an' he was troubled with bears, one spring. Lost a couple o' shoats out of his pen, an' found the tracks o' bears, but couldn't ketch up with 'em to shoot 'em. Three or four nights he heard 'em prowlin' 'round the buildin's, scarin' the stock, an' every time he'd run out with the gun, they'd be gone. Finally he thought up a smart plan. He got his boys to build some little wooden troughs, an' set 'em out, 'round the clearin'. He'd made plenty o' sugar an' syrup, so he took a mess of it an' mixed in the half of a gallon jug o' Medford rum—the kind everybody had in the house, them days. Then he put the stuff in the troughs an' went to bed. When daylight come, he looked out, an' there was a funny sight. An old she-bear an' two cubs was rollin' an' staggerin' around the place, drunk as lords. Soon as he could stop laughin' he went out an' shot the big one. The boys kept the cubs fer pets."

There was a chuckle from Ben Buckalew. "Judge," he said, "are ye sure that bear that hed the rasslin'-match with yer Uncle Lemmie wa'n't in the same condition?"

When the laughter had died down, Judge Garland gave the ladle to Dan. "Keep a-stirrin' an' pourin' it," he advised. "That's the only way to git syrup fit to put on flap-jacks as good as Debbie's."

He went back to the circle and sat down on a log.

"Saw Eph Hayes haulin' hay again, today," he announced. "Runnin' short o' feed fer his stock, I guess, an' has to buy it. Eph ain't as provident as his great-grandfather was. Ever hear about ol' Jeems Hayes in the starvin' year? Prob'ly you have, Jotham, an' you, Ben. It's quite a yarn, an' true, every word.

"The year 1816 was known all over this part o' the country as the starvin' year. Hundreds o' families was close to dyin', an' many did die, I reckon. That year they never had no real summer. The town records in Dover tell about it. Middle o' May the ground was still froze hard enough to bear a man. They had heavy frosts right through June, an' on the fifteenth there was ice on the tan-yard pond. Middle of August it snowed on the high ground, an' by the end of August there was killin' frosts that ruined what corn an' apples had come through.

"Only one man in the state o' New Hampshire seemed to prosper, an' that was Jeems Hayes. He had a corn-field—mebbe a dozen acres—that flourished like the green bay tree. No frost touched it. By fall he husked a good many hundred bushel o' big yellow ears, stored 'em safe in his barn, an' sat back to wait. Folks was still superstitious in them days, an' some of 'em claimed he must be in league with the devil to git off so well. I've always figgered he was jest a good, smart farmer with a little luck.

"Well, soon as winter come, the starvin' began. Farmers hadn't been able to save any crops, an' lots of 'em hadn't any money to buy food. Those that did drove down to Jeems Hayes' place and begged fer corn. If they had hard silver dollars they got it—one dollar a peck. Paper money wouldn't do. He had to be paid in silver. One feller come forty miles to buy corn, an' then had to go twenty more to change his greenbacks into cartwheels.

"They say by the time the corn was all sold, old Jeems had a whole trunkful o' silver dollars, an' was pretty well hated by everybody in the middle counties."

The old gentleman paused and Dan stopped stirring long enough to ask a question. "What became of all that money, Grandpa?" said he. "They must have been rich, for those times."

"You keep that ladle goin', an' I'll tell you 'bout it," the Judge replied sternly. "That's another story an' a pretty interestin' one. Old Jeems Hayes never spent a penny of it. He died pretty soon after the starvin' year. Seems he had a grandson that was a wild youngster. One night the boy brought a crowd of his cronies to the house an' they was drinkin' and carousin'. His mother got to worryin' about that silver, thinkin' they might steal it. So she put all she could carry in a big bag an' went tip-toein' out. She was a powerful stout woman, fer she lugged that silver two or three miles into the woods. Finally she come to a place where there was three big trees growin' close together, an' there she dug a hole an' buried it.

"After a few days she decided 'twould be safer back home, so she set out to find it. Everything looked different. There was so many big trees, an' all of 'em seemed to be growin' three in a bunch. She told the neighbors about it an' they hunted. Fer years every boy in the township tried to find that treasure. I know I had many a crack at it. You see, the place she thought she'd been, that night, was right up here in the Garland Pines."

"Sa-a-ay!" gasped young 'Lysses, "is that right—honest?"

Jotham Grant nodded. "I reckon 'tis," he said. "I've often heard my pa tell about it, an' he said Mis' Hayes was positive she'd buried it right up on the knoll."

"And nobody ever found it?" asked Dan.

"Don't b'lieve so," his grandfather answered. "Never heard about it if they did, an' no one 'round here ever turned up sudden-like with their pockets full o' silver dollars. Danny, lemme look at that syrup."

He took the ladle and expertly poured a stream of the hot liquid from high in the air into the kettle. "Gittin' mighty close to the finish," he said. "Better have some crocks ready, Jotham."

Ten minutes later the syrup, thick and clear, was poured steaming into big earthenware jars and set in the shed to cool. Dan wrapped a five-pound chunk of the sugar they had made that morning in a paper bundle and stowed it in the cutter as a present for Debbie. Then he and his grandfather started back to Green Hill. The sleighing was poor, and in spots where bare ground showed they had to drive on the snow at the side of the road. The Judge let the little mare take her time. He had plenty of things to talk about.

"Jeff Newcomb an' I did business," he said with a chuckle. "The market on first grade square-edge pine was thirty dollars a thousand foot. I'm gittin' thirty-two fer all o' mine, an' twenty-one fer the box-boards. You see Jeff had seen the Garland Pines—knew what clean, choice lumber they'd make. We're to begin shippin' soon as Buckalew can git it hauled to the railroad. Ben's got three farmers lined up to start loadin' fer us right away, an' they'll keep at it till their spring work commences. By the end o' March we ought to have at least ten carloads on the way—mebbe three hundred thousand foot o' pine. That's eight or ten thousand dollars cash money, boy. More'n I've seen fer many a day, an' jest the beginnin' o' what we're goin' to have."

They drove through the gate and in the open barn door. As Dan unharnessed, he heard Debbie's shrill voice telling the Judge what she thought of folks who didn't come home for supper. An entire pot of beans, he gathered, as well as a specially nice loaf of brown-bread with raisins in it, had been wasted. Likewise a jar of piccalilli had been opened and would probably spoil.

Hastily the boy put Babe in her stall and took the package of maple sugar out of the sleigh. The Judge had beaten a retreat when Dan got to the kitchen, and the housekeeper was ready for a fresh victim, her eyes snapping and her arms akimbo.

With a disarming grin he went straight up to her. "Don't say it, Debbie," he laughed. "There was only one thing would make me miss one o' your Saturday night suppers, an' that was so I could bring you this." He thrust forward his peace-offering, and Debbie's wrath melted at the sight.

"Well, I declare!" she said. "Real maple sugar! Maybe them beans'll be all right warmed up, an' I'll see if I can't save the piccalil'. I guess 'twas worth it, Danny, after all."

<h1 style="text-align:center">XVI</h1>

MARCH came in with another snow—"a lumberman's snow," Ben Buckalew called it. There was enough to insure good sleighing for the next few weeks, but it fell gently, without drifting.

Each day now the big bob-sleds of the haulers jingled in and out of the pasture and a steady stream of fragrant white lumber moved to the railroad siding, three miles away. But almost as fast as it was hauled out, new piles sprang up in the sticking-field. Twenty-two thousand feet a day was no novelty by this time. The mill had sawed as high as twenty-four thousand in one eleven-hour stretch, to set a new record.

In the woods the Frenchmen worked tirelessly, felling the big trees. There was no let-up in their rivalry. Dan, swinging ax and saw with either crew that needed him, kept a sort of perpetual contest going. He had the teamsters make a tally of the logs they hauled from each cutting in the course of a day. At the end of the week he would total up the count and tack the paper in a prominent place inside the bunk-house, where it could be seen and discussed during the day of rest. As a result both Duquette and Brosseau would have their men out of bed and ready for the woods at the first peep of dawn on Monday.

Tim Gargan abetted Dan nobly in his efforts. The one-eyed Klondiker had an uncanny skill at concocting dishes dear to the lumberjack's heart. Each Saturday night, when the pork and beans were disposed of, he would bring forth a special dessert and place it with ceremony before Big Pete or Leo Duquette —whichever had set the pace that week. The rest of the crew might grumble, but all they got was pie.

Before the middle of March the sawing passed two million feet. The Garland pines were little more than a memory now.

Used as Dan was to the changed appearance of the timber-lot, he got a lump in his throat sometimes, when he looked across those desolate acres of stumps and brush. A narrowing rank of tall pines still reared their heads gallantly along the far side of the knoll. On its summit stood the old giant, like a beleaguered monarch surrounded by the faithful remnant of his guard.

When the boy remembered the cool, solemn hush

of those woods in summer, the shadowy aisles with dapples of sunlight flecking their smooth brown floor, the sight of the slashing made him homesick. He wondered if the money they got out of it could ever pay for the destruction of such loveliness.

Nevertheless the money was welcome. Before the end of March a dozen flat cars, loaded with Garland lumber, had gone to Boston. The first check was for eleven thousand dollars. The Judge paid Buckalew a substantial sum on account, bought himself a new buggy-whip, and put the rest in government bonds. As Debbie said, he was "proud as a boy with his first long pants."

"You know, Danny," he told his grandson, at breakfast, one Sunday morning, "I could ha' sold the farm up there, with the timber, fer forty thousand. That was two years ago. Some folks thought I was stubborn not to sell. But this lumber's goin' to net us close to sixty thousand dollars, an' we still own the land. By the time you're my age it'll grow another crop o' nice white pine, just like I told you. Yes, sir! It pays to be far-sighted when you're dealin' in timber."

Debbie's mouth was grim as she set a platter of ham and eggs before the old gentleman. "My experience o' far-sighted folks," she said, "is that they're always countin' chickens 'fore they're hatched."

Dan laughed. "You can't scare us now, Debbie," he told her. "The sawing's pretty nearly done, and there's better than two million feet of lumber up there in the pasture, ready to haul."

"I know," she answered. "Things've been goin' too smooth. 'Tain't natural. Gives me an uneasy feelin'."

Around the first of April there came an unseasonable dry spell. Usually that period of the spring was known as "mud-time," and fully justified its name. But this year when the snow went it was followed by sun and warm winds that dried the mud and sent clouds of gray dust whirling among the leafless roadside trees.

The men who had been hauling lumber to the cars found the ground dry and left at once to do their spring plowing. Jotham Grant reported his well was running low. One or two farmers were already having to borrow water from their neighbors.

"I don't like the looks of it," he told Dan one evening. "We need rain worse'n any spring I recollect. Goin' to be bad fer crops unless we git a good long wet spell soon. Look at that sunset. Forest fires all 'round to the south an' west of us."

In the murky haze that shrouded the horizon the

sun was a disc of dull blood-red. "Well," said Dan, "at least we don't have to worry much about that. There's only two or three hundred thousand feet left to cut."

He looked up across the pasture, where acre on acre of gleaming new board-piles stood in orderly rows. It had been a big job but it was nearly done now. And he felt a comfortable pride as he thought of his own share in its accomplishment.

Even if those distant forest fires should sweep nearer, he reflected, there was little danger to the sawn lumber. The prevailing wind for the last few days had been from the south. And on that side, beyond the old stone wall, there were wide tilled fields. To the north and west, plenty of open pasture lay between the lumber piles and the cut-over area.

Next day there were clouds in the sky but the south wind still blew and the smoke haze thickened. Dan could catch its pungent smell as he worked in the sticking-field. He felt sorry for the owners of that timber that was burning. Two or three times, in other years, he had been called out with the neighbors to fight woods-fires, and he knew how fast the red destroyer could roar through a valuable piece of standing pine.

When the chores were done that night, Jotham

Grant sniffed the air before going in. "Seems to me there's less smoke," he said. "Wind's shifted off a mite to the east. Good sign. Air feels more like rain, an' I shouldn't wonder if we'd git it, 'bout tomorrer."

Dan undressed and went to bed. Handling green planks all day had made him tired. He dropped into deep slumber the instant his head touched the pillow.

Hours later he was roused by a persistent shaking at his arm. "Danny!" 'Lysses' voice was shouting. "Wake up, quick! I think there's a fire!"

Dan struggled upward, blinking at a red glow that danced and brightened on the slanting rafters. Then with a bound he was out of bed, running to the rear window. The mill and the bunk-house stood in black outline against a background of ruddy smoke and leaping flames. Faint shouts were mingled with another sound—a low, crackling roar.

"Wake your father!" yelled Dan, and pulled on his clothes, his fingers clumsy with haste. In another minute he was downstairs. He grabbed up a shovel from the tools in the shed and raced up the lane. The fire, he saw as soon as he reached the pasture, was blazing in the brush and high grass that grew in a narrow strip along both sides of the southerly wall. The dry stuff burned like tinder, shooting flames high in the air and licking outward on the wind to touch the nearest piles of lumber, only a dozen yards away. Black figures of men ran and jumped before the blaze like demons of the pit. The whole crew was there, armed with axes, shovels, blankets drenched in the precious trickle of water that was now the brook.

Buckalew, cool as ever, stood behind them shouting his commands.

"Git them wet blankets over the board-pile," he yelled. "Further down—all the way to the ground. Mel, you an' Bill Bean start throwin' that second pile back, so it won't ketch from this one! Duquette! Back of ye! Grass afire!"

Dan ran forward with his shovel, to help half a dozen men who were fighting the stubborn blaze in the dead grass along the wall. The heat was scorching, and there was a constant menace from flying sparks of brush. One or two of the Frenchmen, Dan saw, had rolled in the brook to wet their clothes.

At first he tried to throw dirt on the flames, but the pasture sod was hard to cut, and he found the fire gaining on him. There was nothing for it but to beat and beat with the flat of the shovel.

The battle-line was moving westward now, as the conflagration followed the wall up-hill, fanned by the wind. Three stacks of lumber at once were afire despite the efforts of the mill-crew to smother the flames.

Dan wiped the sweat from his eyes before returning to the attack. A bitter sense of helplessness seized him. If the fire ever got a start he knew nothing could save the fortune in pine boards that lay there in the pasture.

Suddenly at his shoulder he heard a familiar voice.

"Danny—git an ax an' bring that shovel. We've got a job to do!"

It was his grandfather, bareheaded, his white hair flying in the wind. Dan ran, stumbling, to the bunkhouse and picked up an ax. The old man was already hurrying westward between the lumber-piles. He caught up with him at the upper side of the sticking-field.

"I saw the red in the sky an' knew it was close," panted the Judge. "Come up fast as the mare could travel. You 'n' me ain't no use here. These fellers'll take care o' the lumber. But look!"

He pointed toward the knoll and the tall pines ahead of them. The fire had reached the slashing and was already raging westward through the scattered heaps of brush.

"Got to head her off 'fore she reaches the ol' pine up there," he gasped, and ran on, picking his way between the stumps.

Dan saw what he meant. He knew that to the old

man the greatest tragedy that could befall them would be to lose the big double pine—grand-daddy of all the timber on the farm.

They got to the knoll with only minutes to spare. The flames were rolling up the slope, finding plenty of fuel in the dry brush-piles left from the cutting. Smoke, shot with blazing sparks, came over in suffocating clouds. Dan ran to the nearest heap of brush and hurled it back in the direction of the fire. He had to clear as wide a space as possible between the fire and the standing trees before the flames overtook him. Working with furious speed, he threw back the masses of dry pine boughs that littered the ground. Saplings fell under a single stroke of his ax and followed the brush. He could feel the fierce heat of the fire now, and hear the crackle of the oncoming flames. But he was making headway. A cleared zone, twenty to thirty yards wide, gave protection to the trees across almost the whole front of the threatened area. Almost!

From up by the double pine came an anguished cry. "Dan! Quick!"

He saw his grandfather beating feebly with the shovel at a leaping flash of flame. The fire had broken through at one spot where brush still lay and raced to the very foot of the giant tree. Dan ran up the hill

DAN RAN UP THE HILL WITH ALL THE STRENGTH HE
HAD LEFT

with all the strength he had left. The earth was soft under his feet. Softer than it had been in the pasture. It could be dug, he thought. Seizing the shovel from the old man's hand he plunged it in the dirt and tossed a great shovelful on the nearest tongue of fire. It stifled the flame's advance. He threw on another and another, digging as he had never dug before. The Judge had picked up a pine branch and was using it like a flail, striking at the wind-blown embers that crackled about his feet. Dan kept on shoveling. The flames roared high and snarled vindictively but they came no closer.

Then, with sudden horror, the boy saw his grand-father stagger and pitch forward, straight into the fire. It took him only a second to spring after him, but flames were already licking at the old man's clothes. Dan caught his feet, dragged him back. His sleeve and the front of his jacket were on fire. In-stantly the boy fell on top of him, smothering the flames with his body, beating them out with his hands.

The Judge's eyes were shut, his face strangely white, his hair and beard scorched and blackened. Dan shook him. "Grandpa!" he cried. "What's the matter? Can't you speak to me?"

There was no answer. The old man lay like one dead. Desperate, Dan picked him up and started along the hill to the left. The fire was burning itself out in the brush-piles, but there was no chance to cut across the still-blazing stump land. He had to go around, to the north, where no fire had been. The Judge's hundred and sixty pounds made an awkward load, and Dan had been dog-tired when he started. Twice he stubbed his toe and nearly fell. It was hard to see where he was going, and he grumbled to himself at the failing light, until he realized what it meant. The fierce glare of the fire, which had made everything as bright as day, had subsided now to a blackness broken by a few patches of glowing embers. And it was raining! How long those cold drops had been beating on his face and hands he could not tell, for he had been staggering onward as if in a dream.

Voices came to him from the right, somewhere down in the pasture. "Hey! Dan! Judge Garland!" There was a glimmer of light from a moving lantern.

"Here!" Dan croaked. "Up this way!" And suddenly his legs refused to hold him any longer. He was sitting on the ground, holding the limp form of his grandfather in his arms when they found him.

It was Tim Gargan who carried the lantern. With him were Pete Brosseau and 'Poleon Duval. The two Frenchmen picked up the Judge between them, Brosseau taking his shoulders and the marker holding his legs with that potent single arm. Tim helped Dan to stand up and they started for the buildings.

"Well," said the cook, "we didn't lose much after all. The edges of about four piles o' lumber got burnt —mebbe a couple o' thousand foot. What happened to the Judge?"

Dan told him in a few words. "I don't think he's badly burned," he said, "unless he swallowed some flame. What I'm worried about is his heart. Grandpa's a pretty old man to work the way he did tonight."

Buckalew met them at the mill. "Who is it—the Judge?" he asked. "I was afraid o' that."

He made a hurried examination, by the light of the lantern. "The burns ain't dangerous," he announced. "'Pears to me like a stroke or somethin'! Dan, we've got to git him to a hospital, fast as we can take him. Here's the Judge's mare, all hitched. I'll drive ye both down to Riverdale."

They wrapped the old gentleman in a blanket and placed him in Dan's arms, where he sat in the buggy. Then Buckalew took the driver's seat.

"Jotham," he called, as he picked up the reins, "I'll leave it to you to telephone the sheriff. That fire was set, sure's yer a foot high, an' I know who done it. An' this time, by thunder, we're goin' to ketch him!"

XVII

DAN NEVER forgot that ride. The beating rain drummed on the buggy-top and gleamed on Babe's black flanks. The little mare trotted fast despite the darkness, picking her sure-footed way through the puddles. Before they had gone a mile the old man stirred in Dan's arms and murmured something. Then with a long sigh he fell asleep.

"That's better," said Buckalew. "He's breathin' natural now. We'll pull him through, boy—don't you worry."

They drove on a while in silence, before the lumberman spoke again. "I'm anxious to git back there," he said, "soon's we make the Judge comfortable. I'm as certain as I ever was of anything that Daggett set that fire. Only this time we've got to have proofs. I'm goin' to put that devil in jail if it's the last thing I do. Grant's dog was barkin', 'round midnight. I set out to git up, but he quieted down pretty soon, an' I figgered 'twas nothin' but a fox passin', or some other critter. Then, first thing I knew, that brush by the wall was afire. Mebbe you don't know it, but we had a close call, son."

"I thought Daggett was in Canada," said Dan wearily.

"Prob'ly was," the mill-man answered. "He's been layin' low up there fer three months. But he's the kind o' skunk that keeps a grudge. When this dry spell hit, an' he heard about the forest fires, he come sneakin' back, seein' a chance to git even with all of us."

Long before they reached Riverdale, Dan's arms were aching and his legs were numb from the old man's weight. But at last the scattered street-lights came in view. It was four o'clock in the morning when they pulled up before the hospital. With the help of a sleepy attendant they carried the Judge to a private room and saw him put to bed. The physician who examined him gave them cheerful news.

"No, he hasn't had a stroke," he said. "And the burns on his face and arms ought to heal up without any great trouble. You say he was fighting a timber-fire? Probably just exhaustion. His pulse is weak, but his heart's all right—or will be when he's had a few days' complete rest."

They arranged for a private nurse to stay with the Judge for the first twenty-four hours, and gave the hospital the telephone number in Green Hill, so that frequent reports might be relayed to Debbie.

Then, after a cup of coffee and some ham and eggs at an all-night lunch, they set out for the woods again. The rain continued steadily. A dark dawn had merged into a gray morning when they stopped at the Garland house. Debbie was in a state. She had been up ever since the Judge's departure worrying about what might happen to him. But once she knew the worst she took it with stoical New England calm.

"I'll go down tomorrow an' see he's well took-care-of," she announced. "Nobody knows but me what he likes to eat. An' I reckon soon's he begins to feel better he'll be hollerin' fer vittles. Mebbe you'll admit I was right, now, Danny, when I told ye things had been goin' a sight too smooth. Somethin' like this is jest what I expected."

They reached the camp before eight, and as soon as Babe was fed and stabled, Dan went with Buckalew to see what they could find about the cause of the fire. It had started on the south side of the wall, some fifty yards west of the bunk-house and stable. The blaze had been fanned westward by the wind and had left the brush and grass behind it untouched. Their first discovery was one to stir any decent man's wrath.

As they passed the bushy thicket that lined the old wall, a whimper came to them from its depths. Dan hastily parted the branches and gasped with anger and pity at what he saw. Lying on the red-stained earth was Jack, the Grants' faithful collie. Blood oozed from a terrible gash in his shoulder and one foreleg was stretched at an awkward angle, obviously broken. A yard or two away lay a cant-hook. Its steel point was darkened with an ugly stain which the rain had not completely washed away.

Buckalew swore to himself grimly. "Pore old feller," he muttered. "Done his best to warn us. Go git one o' my blankets, Dan. We got to carry him home an' see if he can be saved."

Tim Gargan, emptying garbage behind the bunk-house, saw the boy running and asked what was the trouble. "The dirty son-of-a-gun!" he growled, when Dan told him. "Here, lemme see the dog. I've got sort of a way with 'em."

It was only a short distance to the bunk-house, and placing the injured collie carefully on the blanket they carried him there.

"I've nursed many a hurt sled-dog," explained the old Klondiker, as he worked deftly to staunch the flow of blood from the wound. "My leader got in a fight with three timber-wolves once. He was worse off 'n this feller, but I cured him. Easy now, boy, I ain't goin' to hurt ye. Let's see this leg."

With gentle hands, the cook pulled the broken bones straight and snapped them into place. The dog did not move or cry out. Only his labored panting and the suffering in his eyes betrayed the pain he had endured. When it was over, he thrust his nose out feebly in an effort to lick Gargan's hand.

"Better leave him right here, where I can 'tend to him," said the one-eyed man, looking with satisfaction at the splint he had bound on the broken leg. "We'll have him chasin' woodchucks with young 'Lysses, 'fore hayin'-time."

Back at the wall, Dan found Buckalew kneeling beside the edge of the burnt-over area. In his hand was the end of a partly consumed match, and he was studying a scrap of newspaper that lay in the sodden ashes.

"See what ye make o' that, Danny," he said, pointing to the paper. The boy knelt and looked at it closely. It was only a fragment from the lower corner of a page, the main part of the sheet having been burned away. Two or three insignificant news paragraphs, made half illegible by smoke and rain, were all that showed. It was the date-lines of these items that caught Dan's attention.

"Quebec, Apr. 6," one of them read. And another began, "Sherbrooke, Apr. 6."

"April sixth," said Dan. "Today's the ninth, isn't it? This paper probably came out on the seventh—two days ago. And it was published in Canada—Montreal, I should think."

"That's about the way I figgered it," nodded the mill-man. "Better leave it just as it is for the sheriff to see. He'll be here any time, now. Only one thing—we've got seven or eight Canucks right here in camp. 'Most any of 'em might have had a home paper sent in. You an' I know none of our boys done this, but as evidence in a court o' law—"

"Wait," said Dan. "I don't believe Brosseau or Cantillon or any of the woods-crew can read English. They get Montreal papers—sure. But they're all printed in French. I've seen 'em."

"That's right!" Buckalew exclaimed. "Then mebbe this piece, here, *is* important. There was a burnt match beside it, an' there ain't a bit o' doubt in my mind that it was used to light the grass an' bushes. If only he'd left some tracks! But I looked fer them first of all, an' there wa'n't a sign anywhere 'round."

There was no sawing done, that day. The men, exhausted with their long night battle, were allowed to sleep most of the morning. And there were hours of work to be done in the afternoon, sorting the damaged lumber from the piles, collecting scattered tools, and cleaning up the débris.

At three o'clock 'Lysses came home from school and at once rushed up to the bunk-house, pale with anxiety over his dog. Reassured by Gargan's cheery news, he sought out Dan.

"Pa wants to know where ye took his shovel last night," the youngster grinned. "I'm s'posed to go git it."

"Gee, I'd forgotten all about that shovel," said Dan contritely. "You'll find it up at the foot of the old double-trunk pine. There's an ax there, too, that you'd better bring down."

Twenty minutes later Dan saw the boy running across the pasture like mad. He had neither shovel nor ax, but he was gasping for breath and his eyes fairly popped with excitement.

"Danny!" he shrieked. "Look! Look what I found!"

He held out his hand, releasing the tightly clutched fingers, and there in the palm lay two broad discs of metal. Dan stared at them—took one in his hand. It was an old-fashioned silver dollar. He scraped away the crust of black woods-loam that clung to it, and read the minted inscription. The date stood clear— 1811.

"Golly, 'Lysses!" breathed Dan. "You know what you've found? It's the money that woman buried, after the starving year! Where was it?"

"Come on—I'll show ye!" answered the youngster. "These was right where you'd been diggin' last night. When I picked 'em up I didn't stop to see if there was any more."

They crossed the pasture and threaded their way through the blackened stump-land to the knoll. At the top of the ridge the old pine flung its two giant arms skyward—a figure of triumph. And not a dozen yards from its foot a black line marked the limit of the fire's advance. Dan saw the shovel, lying where he had thrown it when his grandfather had collapsed. Close by was a ragged hole in the earth, a yard across, and a foot or more in depth.

Staring into it, both boys were disappointed. Only the dark, muddy loam showed there. Hastily Dan seized the shovel and began digging. The third time he thrust it down there was a clinking sound. A stone? No, as he raised the shovelful of earth, silver gleamed in the hole. 'Lysses fell to his knees and triumphantly brought up four—five—six silver "cartwheels."

After that they forgot the shovel and dug with their hands—"like a couple o' dogs at a woodchuck hole," as 'Lysses put it afterwards. The money came up in handfuls—all alike. Every coin was a silver dollar, and there were literally hundreds of them piled on Dan's coat when they finished.

At last it was clear that the store was exhausted. Dan dug a foot or so in each direction to make certain, then stood back, panting from his labors.

"I thought the Judge said 'twas in a bag," said 'Lysses, lifting a handful of silver and letting it run through his fingers.

"Probably it was," Dan answered. "A gunny sack would have rotted away long ago. A hundred years —gosh!

"What I'd like to know," he added, when he had caught his breath, "is about the three trees. There's a mound here where the stump of one might have stood. And the big pine was right where it is now, of course. But I don't see any sign of a third tree."

"Bet I can tell what happened," offered 'Lysses. "In the dark, she couldn't see but what the ol' double pine was two of 'em. That's why all the folks that hunted fer it afterwards got fooled!"

"You might be right, at that," Dan nodded. "Now how do we go about getting this home?"

By tying the sleeves and corners of his jacket together, he finally improvised a bag in which the heap of silver could be carried. They slung it on the shovel handle and each took one end.

"Golly, Peter!" grumbled 'Lysses, before they reached the head of the lane. "Whoever said that woman was stout didn't tell the half of it. She must ha' been a reg'lar hoss!"

They carried their treasure into the farmhouse kitchen and opened it before Mrs. Grant's astonished eyes. "Say," exclaimed 'Lysses, as they counted the pile. "Who does this money b'long to, anyhow? I thought you an' me would own it, Dan, but mebbe we'd ought to give it to Eph Hayes. 'Twas some ancestor o' his that got it out o' the poor starvin' folks' hides!"

"The thing to do," said Mrs. Grant, "is keep it safe till the Judge gits well. He'll know what's the lawful way to dispose of it."

There were 810 coins in the heap. They packed them in a stout box and put it under their bed in the garret. Then they promptly forgot buried treasure, for more important matters were afoot. The sheriff and two deputies had just driven into the yard.

XVIII

Running downstairs, Dan met the officers as they climbed out of their two-seated buckboard. The horse-faced deputy, Loomis, was the first to greet him.

"Lessee," he said, with a professional frown, "you're young Garland, ain't you? I b'lieve it was a gent name o' Buckalew wanted to see us."

"Yes," said Dan. "Is this the sheriff?"

"Sheriff Whittaker himself, in pusson," answered Loomis importantly, and gestured toward a short, stout man with a pleasant, weather-browned face.

"Howdy, son," smiled the sheriff, putting out a gnarled hand. "Hear you had a fire. Want to show us where 'twas?"

"I'd better get Mr. Buckalew first," said Dan. "It'll only take a minute. You might drive up the lane there, and we'll meet you."

He ran to the mill and located the boss. In another moment or two they were showing the county officers the place where the fire had started. Sheriff

Whittaker listened attentively, his mild brown eyes taking in every detail of the scene.

"This piece o' paper here—I put a stone on it to hold it where 'twas—" Buckalew was saying, when the sheriff interrupted him.

"Just a second, Ben," he said. "What's that stained place on the ground—under them alders?"

Buckalew told him about finding the wounded dog.

"An' that peavy," remarked Whittaker. "Anybody touched it?"

The mill-man looked at Dan inquiringly. "No," said the boy. "At least, I didn't. We tried to leave everything as it was."

Carefully, the sheriff lifted the cant-hook, using a clean handkerchief, and holding it by the thickest part, near the point. "Sometimes rain don't wash off fingerprints," he explained, apologetically. "Leastways, not if the feller's hands was greasy. I'll take this back with me. Now let's see yer paper."

He agreed with them that it was from a Canadian journal, published on the sixth or seventh of April. "Might be useful," he said, and placed it in a large envelope in his pocket, together with the partly burned match Buckalew had found.

The two deputies had been making a fruitless search for foot-prints or other clews, farther down the wall. When they returned, the party had a look at the burned lumber.

"We-ell," the sheriff commented in his gentle drawl, "you've sure got a lot o' handsome pine sawed up here. Whoever set that fire was either powerful careless, or he wanted to hurt you an' the Judge mighty bad. I'm goin' to leave these boys here to see what they can find, round an' about. First thing I want to do myself is take this peavy back to the office an' see if there's any prints on it. Far as this job's concerned, all we got on Daggett is suspicion, an' we need more'n that. Don't worry, though—he ain't gone any great distance. I've got all the roads out o' the county watched, an' the railroad, too. We'll dig him up, soon as we want him."

"Want him!" stormed Buckalew. "I've been

wantin' him fer six months. There's plenty I'd like to take out o' that rat's hide."

"Steady, now, Ben," the sheriff smiled. "He'll git plenty, if we find any proofs against him. Arson's a pretty serious offense."

He gave some instructions to the deputies, swung up to the front seat of the buckboard, and drove rapidly away. Loomis and his companion were to stay at Grant's that night. They spent the hour or two that remained before sunset in searching the fields and roads around the farm, but Dan noticed that they were on hand promptly when supper-time arrived.

Loomis was impressive at the table. It was amazing how a man could eat as much as he did, and at the same time talk as steadily.

"Now this case," he said, spearing another sugared doughnut with his fork, "—this case prob'ly won't be bafflin', once we've got all the fac's. You folks figger, o' course, that this Daggett done it. Don't ye be too sure. In my years of experience on big cases, I've found it's gener'ly the party nobody suspec's that turns out to be guilty. . . . Yes, ma'am, reckon I will have another cup o' coffee, now you mention it. . . . Well, as I was sayin', this fire may ha' been set by most anybody. A passel o' kids, fer instance, hidin' behind the wall to cook somethin' they didn't want their ma to know they had."

He turned a baleful eye in the boys' direction as he spoke these words. Dan merely scowled in return, but 'Lysses almost strangled on a mouthful of pie.

" 'Tain't likely," said Jotham Grant drily. "Boys 'round here are mostly too tired, time the milkin's over, to do much cookin' after midnight."

The following day—the tenth of April—dawned clear after the rain. It was Saturday, and 'Lysses announced at breakfast that he meant to visit the hackmatack swamp as soon as his chores were done. He wanted to find a couple of his traps that had been lost under the snow. The mill was ready to start sawing again and Dan was glad to return to work. He helped Jotham that morning, sticking lumber.

About eleven, when they were starting a fresh pile at the upper edge of the field, a faint hallo reached them from the mill. Bill Bean was standing outside the saw-pit, waving his arms and beckoning.

"Gosh!" said Dan. "It must be something serious. Do you suppose Grandpa's worse?"

He started at a run for the mill, but Bean was cupping his hands to call again. "Both of ye," came his shout. "You, too, Jotham."

Dan arrived ahead of the farmer and his team,

and saw Ben Buckalew talking with the sheriff. He felt a deep relief. It wasn't about the Judge, after all.

"Come here, Dan," called the lumberman. "Sheriff Whittaker's got some real news. There was finger-prints on that cant-hook, an' they're Daggett's, sure 'nough!"

"No question about it," nodded the sheriff. "We had his prints from the time he was sent to jail. Look's like a clear case now, if we can catch him."

"The sheriff needs some more men," Buckalew put in, "an' I've recommended you an' Jotham Grant fer special deputies. I'm one already. What do ye say, Jotham? Willin' to be sworn in?"

The farmer had just come up. "I sure am," he said, "if it'll be any help catchin' that miser'ble critter."

"So am I," agreed Dan.

"All right," Sheriff Whittaker continued. "I've brought warrants fer his arrest with me, an' I'll leave ye one. Reason I wanted somebody here is that Ben an' me'll have to start for Sanbornville right away. They're holdin' a feller there on suspicion, an' it may be Daggett. Loomis an' Jones have gone off up Blue Job way. Somebody on the Sheep Hill Road saw a man runnin' acrost his field last night an' reported it. If anything turns up while we're gone, call my office an' they'll give ye some help."

Ten minutes later Dan and Jotham were full-fledged officers of the county, and Buckalew had driven off with the sheriff.

"Too near dinner-time to go back to the mill, now," said the burly farmer. "Besides, from what I've seen o' deputies, they don't hold with work, much. What we goin' to use fer fire-arms, Danny? Got to be ready fer action."

Dan had an old 38-caliber revolver, in fair working order, upstairs in his bureau drawer. He brought it down and cleaned it, while Jotham swabbed out his shot-gun. They had just finished loading their weapons, and Dan was at the sink, washing his hands in preparation for lunch, when the door burst open with a bang. In came 'Lysses, out of breath and wild-eyed.

"I saw him!" he gasped.

"Saw who? Speak up plain, boy!" commanded his father.

"Ike Daggett!" answered the youngster. "Over in the swamp. I was down under the bank, fishin' fer a trap. Heard a stick snap in the woods an' looked up. He was goin' along the path, lookin' back of him like he was scared o' somethin'."

"Did he see you?" asked Dan.

"No, he couldn't have," 'Lysses was positive. "I

ducked back below the bank real quick. When I peeked again he was out o' sight. Soon's I was sure he was gone, I put fer home, fast as I could come."

"All right, Dan," said the farmer grimly. "We'll git a bite to eat an' start right away."

"Can I come?" 'Lysses pleaded. "I can show ye where he was."

"No, sir—not fer a minute," his father replied. "This is man's work. I reckon we can find his tracks in that wet ground, without no boys under foot."

Mrs. Grant was flustered by this sudden development, but she hastened to take the corned beef and cabbage out of the pot and set plates for Dan and her husband. In a few minutes they had eaten and were on their way.

The rain had softened the surface of the ground to mud, and it was easy to follow 'Lysses' tracks across the plowed ground and pasture sod.

"Looks like Daggett must have a hang-out, somewheres in the swamp," said Jotham Grant. "This is the second time the boy's seen him there. It'd make a good place to hide. Nobody ever goes there to speak of."

They plodded on in silence till they reached the crest of the pasture hill, with its scattered growth of pines and junipers. There Dan motioned the farmer to stay back while he reconnoitered. From behind a scrubby jack-pine he was able to see the broken-down fence that bordered the low land. There was no living thing in sight except a crow, flapping silently away above the tamaracks. Dan was glad he had kept hidden, for if Daggett were a good woodsman he would recognize the alarm call of a crow and take to cover.

He motioned to Jotham Grant to come on, and they went quickly down the hill. At the fence they paused again. There were two half-hidden paths into the swamp. One ran along the brook-bank. The other followed a twisting course, thirty or forty yards farther in. Both showed marks of use since the rain.

"You take one an' I'll take the other," whispered the farmer. "We'll be in sight of each other, an' if ye find anything, give a whistle like a black-bird. I'll do the same."

They separated, Grant following the path nearer the stream. Dan moved carefully, studying every yard of the trail for foot-prints. They were there—big, hob-nailed boot-tracks heading in both directions. Off toward the brook, between the trees, he could see the farmer, also proceeding slowly.

Little by little, Dan's trail edged to the left into the swamp. There were low places and pools of stagnant water which he avoided by stepping on grass-tussocks. All the trees around him now were the dreary tamaracks, with their pale, drooping mantles of moss. He could catch only an occasional glimpse of Jotham Grant, now some distance away.

Another hundred yards and he had completely lost sight of his companion. Beyond a thicket the path took a sudden turn to the left. And in the moss he found the fresh, distinct print of a man's boot, pointing onward into the swamp. Dan's heart began to beat faster. He had a feeling that their quarry was close, now. Pursing his lips he imitated the soft *oke-a-lee* of a red-winged black-bird. After a few seconds the answering whistle came faintly from the right. The farmer had heard him and would be along in a moment.

The boy broke a twig to show the direction he had taken, and pushed on, along the faintly marked path. He took the revolver out of his jacket-pocket and held it ready. The heavy butt had a comforting feel in his hand. Occasionally he stopped to listen and stare ahead, trying to pierce the sinister shroud of the tamaracks with his eyes.

The bog-holes were more frequent now—black, ugly-looking patches of water, shadowed by tussocks of swamp grass. The trail was harder to find, as it zig-zagged secretly among the trees and pools. Twice Dan broke twigs to give Jotham Grant guidance in following him. He must have proceeded thus for half a mile when he saw a thin wisp of smoke rising beyond a clump of blueberry bushes. He looked back, but the farmer was not yet in sight. Should he wait? So far, he knew he was unobserved, and if he went on alone he thought he could get the drop on the ex-convict. A delay now might give Daggett the advantage.

Casting prudence to the winds he moved forward, stepping almost as quietly as an Indian. Through the brush he could see a low, bark roof, from one end of which a piece of rusty stove-pipe thrust upward. There was a faint scent of wood-smoke in the air, and a low, sizzling noise. The man in the cabin must be cooking something in a skillet.

As Dan came around the blueberry clump he saw that the shack had no windows. There was a door in the end opposite the chimney, and toward this the boy edged his way, the revolver gripped in front of him. He was scared now, wishing he had the support of Jotham Grant. His knees felt wobbly and he was breathing fast. At the corner of the cabin he almost turned back, but anger came, to replace his fear. The man he could hear moving inside had tried to steal

Babe—had cruelly beaten young 'Lysses and left him to freeze—had nearly killed Jack, the collie, and then done his best to burn the Garland lumber.

These thoughts ran through Dan's veins like fire. He felt strong again, and determined. Before him stood the door, ajar. He laid his left hand on it and, suddenly flinging it open, stepped over the threshold.

It was unexpectedly dark, inside. The door struck something—a box or a stool—and knocked it over with a crash. Dan leveled his revolver at a tall shape beside the fire-place. "Put up your hands!" he shouted hoarsely, "I've got you covered!"

The shape did not move. Instead, a heavy stick of wood came hurtling from the side of the room, behind the door, and struck his right wrist with numbing force. The gun flew out of his hand and in the next instant he was grappling with a tall, sinewy man who sprang on him in the half-darkness.

It was Daggett. The daylight from the door showed him the fellow's evil face in their first fierce scramble. Dan knew he was fighting for his life. He wrenched the gripping fingers away from his throat and struggled to one knee, then to his feet.

Daggett swung a wild fist at his jaw but the boy blocked it and plunged in, to grip him with powerful arms around the chest. In weight and strength he was a match for the ex-convict. But his opponent seemed to know tricks of which Dan had never dreamed. Now, as the boy's arms tightened in a bear-hug on his ribs, the ne'er-do-well brought up a knee to foul him painfully. Dan winced and let go his grip. And in that split second Daggett's fist crashed against his eye.

Down he went, his head ringing, but he was able to scramble half-way up before his adversary could kick him. Lunging forward from a crouching position, he rammed his head into Daggett's middle, and they went down together, with Dan on top. All over the earthen floor they fought—kneeing, strangling, gouging, kicking.

Suddenly Daggett pulled free, rolling half-way across the cabin. When he came up it was with the forgotten revolver in his hand. There was murder in his slits of eyes. Murder in the twitching of his finger on the trigger. Dan stayed where he was, waiting through seconds that seemed hours for the shot that would bring oblivion.

"I got ye now!" panted the desperado. "Back out that door—an' don't start nothin' or I'll drill ye."

Dan's palsied legs carried him slowly backward, and Daggett followed, step for step, the muzzle of the gun a bare yard from the boy's breast. When they

ALL OVER THE EARTHEN FLOOR THEY FOUGHT

were both outside the door, a malicious snarl twisted the ex-convict's face.

"Jes keep on backin'," he said. "There's a quicksand hole right behind ye. No—don't look 'round. It's there, all right, an' ye'll find it in about ten more steps. Bog-holes don't leave no stains an' such, to make folks ask questions."

XIX

A WAVE of nausea made Dan weak. It took all the will-power he could command to keep his feet moving back—and back. Shaken with terror, he tried to calculate his chances if he made a dive for Daggett and risked a bullet. The wicked little eye of the gun was very steady, and stared straight at his heart. He took another hesitant backward step, feeling for the ground with his foot.

"Drop that!" came a sudden voice. "Put yer hands high!"

Dan saw Daggett's face turn white. The revolver fell from his grasp and both his arms reached upward. Thirty feet away, by the corner of the cabin, stood Jotham Grant, covering the ex-convict with his shot-gun.

"Now walk over this way a little closer," said the farmer. "Danny, see if there's some rope inside there."

The boy picked up the revolver, his hand still shaking from his ordeal, and went toward the shack. Before he went, however, he looked behind him long enough to see a yawning black swamp-hole not three yards from where he had last stood.

Inside the cabin he stumbled over a rough table, upturned in the battle, and reaching the chimney, he poked up the fire to give more light. The place could hardly be called furnished. A bough bed with a dirty blanket in one corner. A little heap of unwashed cooking utensils on the hearth. A dark overcoat hanging on a nail near the chimney—that was the tall shape Dan had mistaken for a man when he first entered. Nothing like rope or cord was to be seen, but the blanket was new and stout despite its filthy condition. He picked it up and tore it lengthwise into strips. Under one corner was a small package rolled up in a newspaper. It was light and soft to the touch. Dan took it out of the cabin with him.

In another minute or two, Daggett's wrists were securely bound behind him with the strips of the blanket.

"All right," said Jotham Grant. "Keep the critter here an' shoot him if he moves an inch. I'm goin' to look through the place, 'fore we leave. What's that thing you found?"

"I don't know," Dan replied. "It was in the bunk. Open it and see."

Grant unrolled the paper and held up a prime mink skin.

"That's mine," growled the prisoner. "Ye can't take my property!"

"Yours, eh?" said Jotham coldly. "We'll let young 'Lysses tell the court about that. Ought to make an interestin' exhibit fer a jury—this here pelt."

He made a quick inspection of the cabin but found nothing more of importance. He wrapped the mink skin carefully in its paper again and slipped the bundle in his coat pocket.

"Let's be gittin' along," he said. "Dan, you go on ahead. I'll come last. An' don't fergit, you low-down skunk, this gun-bar'l won't be more'n six foot from yer yeller back. Nothin' would give me more pleasure'n to blow yer head off. Git movin'."

Dan led the way along the treacherous trail through the bog. He realized, now that he had more time to look around, how skillful the renegade had been in placing his hide-out. No one ever visited the swamp except occasional berry-pickers in the summer, and they never ventured far beyond its edges. It was only 'Lysses' chance glimpse of the fugitive that had led them to search the place. If the boy had not gone there that morning, Daggett might have remained hidden for months.

They reached the path along the brook and crossed the fence. A shout greeted them as they started up through the pasture. Four armed men were coming down the hill—Sheriff Whittaker, Buckalew and the two regular deputies.

"By thunder, I b'lieve they've got him!" Dan heard Buckalew yell. And a moment later they were shoving their prisoner forward to meet the astonished group.

"So this is the feller, eh?" said the sheriff mildly. "Yeah, I'd recognize him from his Rogue's Gallery picture. What's the matter, son—you have a little trouble?"

This last was addressed to Dan, who up to that moment had forgotten all about his black eye and the rents in his clothes.

"We had sort of a tussle," the boy grinned. "If Jotham hadn't come along, I reckon I'd have been in a bad fix."

Whittaker untied the blanket strips and put a pair of handcuffs on Daggett's wrists. Then they returned across the fields to the Grant farm. The sheriff's buckboard was waiting there, and without further delay they bundled the ex-convict into the rear seat. As the sheriff took his place beside him he smiled down at Jotham and Dan.

"You fellers'll only git one day's pay as special deputies," he said, "but you sure earned it. In a case like this the county pays fifty dollars' reward. Maybe that'll help a little. An' we'll prob'ly want ye both to testify when the Grand Jury's called. Well, so long. We'll take good care o' this bird."

As the buckboard bumped out of the yard, Ben Buckalew laid his hand on Dan's shoulder. "Good job!" he said. " 'Pears to me it'd do yer Grandpa a heap o' good to hear 'bout this. What say you an' me give ol' Major a little exercise this afternoon, an' pay him a call?"

"You bet!" Dan answered eagerly. "I've got to change my clothes and wash some of this dirt off first, though."

As he ran into the kitchen, 'Lysses was holding up the mink skin. "Ain't that a beauty, Dan?" he cried. "I'd know that mink anywhere. He didn't do such an extry job o' skinnin', but it's still a corkin' good pelt."

The piece of newspaper in which it had been wrapped slipped off the table and fluttered to the floor. Dan, stooping to pick it up, gave a sudden exclamation. "Say!" he called. "Jotham, look here! It's a sheet out of a Montreal paper, dated the 7th of April. Remember that burned piece? The sheriff kept it, and he'll be tickled to get this. It ought to give him all the evidence he wants."

Dan bathed his damaged eye, put on a decent suit of clothes and went out to join Buckalew, who was waiting in the buggy. Major was champing at the bit, anxious to go. The boy climbed in and settled himself for the ride. Stiff and sore as his body felt, he was happier than he had been for a long time.

"This has been a good winter," mused the lumberman, as they drove along. "Never cut a piece o' timber that gave less trouble—or had a crew that worked harder. You're a born woods-boss, Dan. Handled 'em perfect. If you wasn't so set on goin' to college I'd offer ye a job right now as foreman. The lumber business ain't what it was, but there'll always be a livin' fer a feller that can run a portable mill."

Dan was pleased. "Maybe I'll take you up on that offer some time," he said. "How much more is there to cut?"

"I shouldn't estimate more'n two hundred thousand," Buckalew replied. "Ten days' sawin', barrin' bad weather an' accidents. We'll pile the brush an' burn it, 'fore we move the mill, an' the teamsters'll be here most o' the summer haulin' the lumber to the cars."

At the hospital in Riverdale, a smiling nurse told

them Judge Garland was feeling much better and could see them for half an hour. The old gentleman was wrapped up in a chair by the sunny window. At his side sat Debbie in her Sunday alpaca, reading him bits from the town paper.

She rose as they entered and advanced upon them, her mouth set in a forbidding line. "Don't you go upsettin' him with no fires an' sech now," she murmured. "I've half a mind not to let ye in here at all."

But the Judge winked at them solemnly over the housekeeper's shoulder, and beckoned them to come closer. "My lands, Debbie," he said, "don't ye know I've been pinin' fer male company? Jest the sight of 'em puts new life in me!"

His voice was weak, but the old spark of humor lit his eyes.

"Come here, Danny, an' let me have a look at ye," he urged. "Hm-m—who ye been tanglin' with?"

They told him the story of Daggett's capture, and he chuckled with delight. "I'm through tryin' to do favors fer that limb o' Satan," he announced. "He'll have to take his medicine now, an' I hope he gits all that's comin' to him. But tell me, boys—the thing that's been frettin' me most is the ol' pine. Did she burn?"

"The pine isn't hurt a bit," grinned Dan. "You

must have put the fire out when you fell into it. Not much of the lumber was burned, either. We got off pretty lucky. And, say—I almost forgot to tell you what 'Lysses found, right at the foot of the big tree!"

As he described the discovery of the silver dollars, the Judge's eyes grew bigger and bigger. "Well, I declare!" he whispered. "Ain't that a caution, though? How much did ye say—eight hundred and ten dollars? Reckon that must ha' been about the whole of it. Folks used to say there was more'n a thousand buried, but I never could believe any woman was strong enough to carry that much. What did ye do with it?"

"We've got it put away in a box under our bed," said Dan. "We didn't know exactly who it belonged to."

"Well," chuckled the Judge, "that *is* a question. 'Twas on our property—land that's been in the Garland family since Revolutionary times. So ordinarily anything we dug up ought to b'long to us—finders-keepers. Then on the other hand we're pretty sure that it was Hayes money once. An' I happen to know Eph Hayes needs cash—as always. Seems to me the fairest way would be to divide it—half to 'Lysses, an' the rest to Eph. Everybody ought to be satisfied, that way."

"That's fine," Dan nodded. " 'Lysses thought perhaps it should all go back to the Hayeses, but he certainly deserves half for finding it."

At the end of thirty minutes the nurse came in and told them their time was up. Debbie collected her hat and coat. "Reckon I'd better go back with ye," she said. "I honestly can't find a bit o' fault with the way they're takin' care of him, an' I s'pose things'll go to rack an' ruin up at Green Hill, if I ain't there to take charge."

She gave a few parting injunctions to the nurse and they bade the old man farewell.

"Don't fret a mite about me," he grinned. "Outside o' gittin' my whiskers singed, I'm as good as ever. An' prob'ly even that was all fer the best. They say it makes the hair grow in thicker. Shouldn't wonder if I come home lookin' like Santy Claus himself!"

Dan spent that night and Sunday at the Garland place. Daylight on Monday found him harnessing Babe for his return to camp. The early mornings were still chilly, those April days, but there was a hopeful smell of spring in the air. Grass was sprouting and buds opening. He heard a bluebird singing in one of the dooryard maples.

By seven o'clock he was at the mill and found

steam already up. With the end of their job in sight, the men worked by the sun, not by the time. Ole Jenson flung a dozen huge slabs into the roaring fire-box and watched the gauge mount. When the needle passed a red mark on the dial he waved a long arm to the sawyer. Whipple spun the valve handle and the engine pistons hissed into action. Up on the skids, Mel Rollins was rolling a thick log toward the carriage. Before it was clamped in place the great saw was purring, and with a shout, the sawyer let in his clutch. The day's work had begun.

Dan went to Buckalew and got his orders. He was to go in with the woods-crew that morning. "We've got a good bright day, an' the boys are rarin' to go," said the boss. "Workin' till sun-down, we've got a chance to break all records. You may be needed with the spare team by afternoon, but git the choppers off to a racin' start first."

The boy's black eye brought forth a few quips from the Frenchmen. Beneath their humor, however, there was increased respect. They had heard about the fight in the cabin and Daggett's arrest, and they accepted Dan now as a man of proved courage.

"Pete," said Dan to Brosseau, as they reached the woods, "it's tough luck for you, but I'm going to work with Duquette this morning. You'd better hump yourself, too, because we're out to set an all-time high mark for chopping. Eh, Leo?"

The diminutive Frenchman laughed delightedly and threw off his jacket. "Here goes!" he cried, and spitting on his hands, he squared off in front of a big pine like David facing Goliath.

All morning they worked like furies. The booming crash of the felled trees came as regularly and almost as rapidly as the guns of a presidential salute. Nobody rested. Nobody had time or breath for words, beyond the panting orders issued by Duquette. At noon they labored ten minutes overtime and only left their work when Brosseau's crew went hurrying by.

"Twelve," called Big Pete. " 'Ow much you mak'?"

"Fourteen!" Dan and Duquette shouted together.

"*Bon!*" laughed the broad-shouldered chopper. "Dat's geeve dose sawyer som'p'n to do, eh?"

But at the mill they found the skids nearly empty. Dan ran to the tally-board and whistled with amazement as he read the figures.

"Twelve thousand eight hundred!" he called to the choppers. "Come on. Eat and get back on the job or they'll catch up with us. Don't let 'em say they had to wait for logs!"

There was little time spent over Tim Gargan's

ALL MORNING THEY WORKED LIKE FURIES

good dinner that day. Within fifteen minutes every man of the crew had bolted his meal and departed. Some did not even stop to light their pipes—an unheard-of omission. Dan knew that the real "neck of the bottle" that afternoon would be the hauling. The bare ground made a heavy pull for the teams, and they had not only been slowed up, as a consequence, but had been bringing down smaller loads. Without eating his pie he made a bee-line for the stable. Old Jerry and Beauty were hustled out of their stalls and into harness. Before the other two scoots had vanished into the woods Dan was trotting his ancient team across the pasture in their wake.

Up beside a pile of Brosseau's logs he drove them and in a moment they were panting back to the mill with two solid sticks of pine on the sled. He was proud of the way they put their spavined old legs into it. "Next time you have a pulling-match," he yelled to Nolan, "count this pair in!"

It was after seven that evening when Dan brought down his final load, in the last of the fading light. At the mill, Joe Whipple was stopping the engine.

"Boy, them cylinders is hot!" he grinned. " 'Poleon, what's the count?"

Duval marked up the tally with a flourish.

"Twenty-five t'ousan', seven hunder' an' twenty!" he announced in his high-pitched sing-song.

"Whew!" Whipple wiped the sweat from his brow with a faded blue sleeve. "Guess that's a day's work to tell about!"

XX

THE MEADOWS were green and the early apple
trees were starting to bloom in the orchards,
when the last of the Garland pine was sawn. The
crew spent three days clearing up the lot and piling
and burning the brush. Then they were ready to move.
It made Dan a little homesick to see the bunk-house
begin to come down. The men had packed their duffel
that morning and it was piled under a tarpaulin on
the rutted ground. Young Cantillon had a happy,
far-away look in his eyes. He was going back to the
goose-girl in Three Rivers, and Raoul Fleury teased
him about it unmercifully.

Dan helped Tim Gargan carry the injured collie
to a wagon and took him down to the farm-house.
The dog's tail began to thump the boards as they
came into the yard. He staggered up on three legs
and gave a feeble bark. He was home again.

By mid-morning the mill shed and the bunk-house
were nothing but neat piles of lumber. The stable
they left, for it would be used by the teamsters that

summer. With a good deal of heaving and straining the mill machinery was loaded on its dray. The boiler and the boss's rolling shanty were pulled and pried out of the deep hollows into which their wheels had settled. The teams were hitched and the cavalcade was ready to start.

Ben Buckalew lolled in his buggy like a gypsy king and cast an eye over the horses. They had had several days of rest and were fit for the twenty-mile pull ahead of them.

"That spare team looks better'n when they come in," the mill-man told Dan. "You've took good care of 'em. If you'd like to earn a little cash this summer I'll lend 'em to ye. I'll pay the same wages I give Nolan an' Couture on this job o' haulin' to the railroad. What say?"

Dan accepted gladly. He wanted to lay by as much money as possible before going to college, and working with his friends the teamsters would be a pleasant way to do it.

"All right, boys?" shouted Buckalew. "Here we go!" And with a creak of gear and a cracking of whips, the wagons began to move. Dan yelled farewells to the crew, as one after another passed him. A hard-bitten crowd, but good men all. Glad as he was to have the big job finished, he hated to see the last of them.

The noise of the wagons grew fainter. The towering dust-cloud faded to a haze far down the road. All that remained was a yellow mountain of sawdust where the mill had stood, and a rutted track across the pasture.

That afternoon he drove to Riverdale to bring his grandfather home from the hospital. The Judge had made a splendid recovery in his two weeks of rest. His cheeks looked as rosy as ever, and his silver hair and beard had been trimmed so that the singed places no longer showed.

"Well, Danny," he said, when they were settled in the road-wagon, "it's all over, is it? To tell the honest truth, I'm sort o' glad I wa'n't there. I talked mighty big about wantin' the pines cut, but I couldn't've watched them last ones come down. They was sort o' like brothers o' mine. Growed up with me."

He looked across the fields contentedly. "Spring sunshine's pretty nice after ye been cooped up indoors a while," he said. Then, after another pause: "Mare's lookin' good an' slick. Too durn fat, though. Wait till I'm a bit stronger, an' I'll trot it off her."

Dan grinned. "Don't you go picking races, now,

Grandpa," he replied. "You're going to take a good rest this summer, while I haul boards. Then in the fall, when I'm in college, you can drive over to Hanover and show 'em what a real trotter looks like."

"Well," sighed the old man, "mebbe this rest business is all right. I ain't ever tried it. Anyway I won't have to worry a lot about money. Sixty thousand dollars! Land's sakes, I never did expect to be wuth that much!

"Say—" he chuckled, "I been thinkin' about that old silver you an' 'Lysses dug up. I sure want to be there when we present Eph Hayes with his share. Eph's picked stone on them bare acres o' his so long, an' always been so hard up, I reckon he'll pop his buttons when we tell him the luck's changed."

So they came over the last hill and swung in between the Garland maples at the mare's prettiest gait. And on the porch was Debbie, her grim face wreathed in smiles, making furtive dabs at her eyes with her apron.

.   .   .   .

When court convened in July, Ike Daggett was tried for arson. To the satisfaction of the entire community, he was convicted, and sentenced to a long term in State's Prison.

Dan went to Dartmouth that fall, tough as nails and ready to play good football. He worked hard in college, took his degree in Science and graduated well up in his class. That June, four years after the Garland timber was cut, he came back to Green Hill for a short vacation before going to work in Boston. And one warm, golden afternoon the Judge said, "Danny, let's take a little ride. I ain't seen the old twin pine since that night we had the fire."

They drove up the winding road past fields that were tall with timothy. Babe, somewhat stiff in the joints when she came out of the stable, limbered up after the first mile and trotted with a smoothness that belied her eighteen years.

"Reckon she'll last as long's I do," smiled the old man. "I don't drive a terrible lot. So many o' these autos on the roads now, it ain't the fun it used to be. Hello—there's 'Lysses!"

A big youngster in overalls grinned at them from Grant's gate. Beside him was an old collie, walking with a limp. The dog looked up at Dan with sad, intelligent eyes, and slowly waved his feathery plume of a tail.

Dan shook hands with the farmer's boy and measured his broad shoulders with an approving eye.

"You're going to be full as big as your Dad, I guess," he said. "Come on with us. We're going up in the old timber-lot."

The mare picked her way along the uneven track through the pasture, and followed the former wood-road beyond. They were able to drive almost to the foot of the knoll. There Dan helped his grandfather down, and very slowly they climbed the rugged hillside.

There was little of beauty here now. The stumps stood bleak and bare in the sun and a riot of young blackberry vines failed to hide the scars of the cutting.

Only at the summit, under the spreading limbs of the old pine, there was shade. Judge Garland eased himself down on the carpet of brown needles.

"There 'tis," he said. "Finest stand o' timber in the state, they used to call it. Looks sort o' measly now, don't it? But, boys, it ain't as bad as it looks. My eyes have gone back on me a little, Danny. Tell me what you see, down there to the west."

Dan laughed. "Not much but stumps and vines and a few little birch saplings, Grandpa," he replied.

"Look closer," the old man insisted. "Down along the ground."

"I see 'em," 'Lysses put in eagerly. "Over there,

Dan. And there—all around. Not much bigger'n yer hand, but they're beginnin' to grow. White pine seedlin's!"

"I thought so," the Judge nodded. "Dig me up one of 'em an' bring it here. I want to see the third generation o' Garland pines with my own eyes."

Dan dug with his fingers around the roots of a tiny seedling and carried it in its lump of earth to place it in the old man's hand.

"Humph!" chuckled the Judge. "Funny little feller, ain't he? Just startin' life, bold as brass. Guess he don't know what a vale o' tears he's gittin' into. Briers an' berry-pickers in the summer, an' blizzards in the winter. Fightin' rocks under foot an' birches overhead to git himself food an' water an' a little sun. He'll make it, though. There's good stuff in these baby pines. They're not quitters. All right, Danny, put him back where you found him."

The Judge sat musing while Dan carefully replanted the little tree. "Well, guess I'm satisfied now," he said, when his grandson returned. "I just wanted to make sure this old-timer here was still doin' his duty. The birches won't hurt the young pines much fer another ten years. Then you can have 'em cut fer cordwood, an' they'll just about cover the taxes. After that the timber'll be able to take care of itself. I reckon you'll be comin' back here off an' on. Folks generally do come back to New Hampshire. They can't stay away, if it's in their blood. You'll have the fun o' walkin' under Garland pines again, an' watchin' 'em grow up straight an' pretty."

Dan stretched his arms thoughtfully. He was remembering the shadows and the quiet in those woods, as he had known them.

"I'll be back, Grandpa," he answered.

A moment later, poking among the needles around the foot of the big tree, he came on a hollow in the ground. " 'Lysses," he said, "I've wondered what you finally did with those four hundred-odd silver dollars."

'Lysses grinned. "Bought me a ram an' six sheep with part of it," he replied. "They're doin' well, too. I've got thirty-five in the flock, this summer. Reckon I'll keep the rest o' the money in bank, an' take a course in Animal Husbandry, down to Durham College, some time."

They helped the old gentleman to his feet and went slowly down the hill. Dan looked back from the pasture bars. The huge twin pine rose on the crest of the ridge, its towering height and mighty spread made more imposing by its loneliness. Age dealt more kindly with trees than with men, thought Dan. There was enduring strength in the upward thrust of the two great trunks. Vigor in the new green of the branches. As long as this tree stood and bore its seed, there would be Garland pines.

THE END